Helmuth Moltke, Mary Herms

Field-Marshal Count Helmuth von Moltke as a Correspondent

Helmuth Moltke, Mary Herms

Field-Marshal Count Helmuth von Moltke as a Correspondent

ISBN/EAN: 9783337383619

Printed in Europe, USA, Canada, Australia, Japan

Cover: Foto ©Andreas Hilbeck / pixelio.de

More available books at **www.hansebooks.com**

FIELD-MARSHAL

COUNT HELMUTH von MOLTKE

AS A

CORRESPONDENT

TRANSLATED BY

MARY HERMS

LONDON

JAMES R. OSGOOD, McILVAINE & CO.

45, ALBEMARLE STREET, W.

1893

CONTENTS.

I.

Letters to His Family.

SELECTIONS FROM LETTERS TO HIS FATHER.[1]

Magadino on Lake Maggiore,
November 2nd, 1840.

On the 22nd of October I left Jena after a month's visit. I took my last bath there in snow, which fell through the open roof into the douche. As we drove through the Thuringian Forest we admired the beautiful snow-laden firs, but on the other side of the hills the snow changed into rain and strong wind. Coburg and Bamberg we passed at night, so I saw but little of this fine country.

On my way, in the dark, from Nuremberg I was not a little surprised to hear a conversation

---

[1] A brief autobiography by his father is included in "Moltke: His Life and Character."

B 2

being carried on in Turkish; but I think the two
Armenians, who were returning from the Leipsic
fair, were no less astonished when I joined in
their chat in the same language. The elder of the
two men was a native of Egin, on the Euphrates.
His heart bounded with joy when I told him that
I knew the villages and mountains of that neighbourhood, and that the Kurds, who had so often
devastated his village, had been defeated, and that
the restoration of the church there was already
begun. He had left his country forty-six years
ago, but still remembered the exact number of
mulberry trees in the vineyard, and what fruit used
to grow on the house. He gave up the house and
garden to his Turkish oppressors, when a boy of
only ten years old, and went to Constantinople,
where, by trade and thrift, he made a fortune.
Jann Karabetha, on his way to the Leipsic fair
a year ago last Easter, was pressed by a Jew to
take a ticket in the Berlin Lottery, and he had
won 50,000 thalers (7500*l.*) His parents died
long ago; his two sisters are both married to
wealthy men in Wallachia; he himself, no longer
young, has neither brothers, wife, nor children.

His one wish is to revisit Merkess, on the Euphrates, once more before his death, and to devote his money to his native village. It was quite touching to hear him describe the assembling of the Echtzar or elders (very likely all buried now), to restore the church; how he would plant trees; introduce wheel-barrows into a country where all burdens were still carried; how he would bring them potatoes, unknown there; construct a plough on wheels, etc. Indeed, such a man would be a real benefactor to his country. Foreign instructors, European politics, the Hattisherif of Gulhane, are not what the country needs, but the wheel-barrow and the potato. But all these plans can only be realized when security is given to life and property, and such security is not to be found on the Euphrates, still less so since the defeat of the Turkish army has allowed the Kurds to return to their old habits of plundering. As things are, I had to advise the Armenian to wait patiently and hope for better times, which, however, I fear he will hardly live to see.

I must leave Armenia, and return to Swabia,

this beautiful country of forests, meadows, villages with picturesque mills, old castles, and cheerful looking little towns. Elwangen, to begin with, is one of the prettiest places to be seen, with its fine castle, and big convent with towers and shrines. In Würtemberg the roads are well kept, but badly planned. They seem to follow the direction of the old bridle roads which led to the castles of the robber knights on the tops of the basalt mountains of Rechberg, Staufen, and Hohentwiel. The heights seem to be chosen purposely, even in the beautiful Rems valley, which runs straight along for ten miles; hills are ascended, only to be descended on the other side, by the help of drags. This would matter little for those who travel merely for pleasure, but the life of the post-horses in Würtemberg is a dreadful one.

Where the Rems flows into the Neckar the valley is wide and most beautiful. Here stands the lovely little town of Cannstadt with a magnificent bridge over the river, which rushes over a long weir through fertile fields and by villages with stately churches and towers. The modern castle of Rosenstein, built in imitation of the

antique style, overlooks the town, which lies in a
deep basin surrounded by high hills. These hills,
crowned with ruins of old castles, are clothed
with vineyards to the height of several hundred
feet, and dotted with the little white cottages of
the vine-dressers.

A fine road, planted on both sides with high
poplars, runs through some plantations for about
half an hour's distance as far as Stuttgart. In
many respects I prefer the capital of Würtemberg
to the much-admired capital of Bavaria. In the
latter everything has been done by the king, in the
former by the inhabitants ; and the situation of
Stuttgart is as fine as that of Munich is desolate.
Stuttgart occupies the whole basin of a deep valley;
the hills rise immediately behind the houses, clad
up to their summits with vineyards. No fields or
meadows are to be seen here ; the town seems to
live upon nothing but grapes. It was just the
vintage time, and the evening twilight was lit up
now and then by rockets. One of the best things
at Stuttgart is the hotel Marquardt, where I refreshed myself thoroughly after three nights spent
in a postchaise.

My first visit was to the high tower of the Stiftskirche, whose two hundred and fifty steps it is well worth while to ascend. The view from the top is most extensive, and greatly facilitates the finding of one's way afterwards. Next I visited the old castle, a fine stronghold, with big round towers and magnificent arcades in the castle yard. In olden times the people of this country not only liked to build their dwellings on the highest hills, but they also liked to live in the highest storeys. An old Count of Würtemberg had stairs built up to the fourth storey, which could be ascended on horseback ; a stone by the door served for mounting and dismounting. On the ground floor is an arena where the tournaments used to be held. The new castle is a finer building, in proportion to the size of the country, than that at Christiansborg, where the state cannot afford the heating of the rooms.

In the morning I drove to Cannstadt, where I had a delicious bath in the mineral waters. They spring to the height of two feet from a marble shell. The water has a pleasant taste. After the parade I visited the Royal stables, where two hundred and fifty stallions are kept. My fancy was taken by some thoroughbred Arabs, small white horses, just fourteen hands, by whom, from English mares, the biggest horses have been bred. While I was admiring them the king passed. He likes to visit his stables from time to time, and though visitors are not allowed, he bowed courteously to me.

Going by Tübingen, which is also very prettily situated, I reached Basle early in the morning, and I went on at once to see the Falls. I will spare you a description of this marvel of nature; one might as well try to describe music as a waterfall. Everyone has read so much about the Falls of the Rhine before seeing them, that the spectacle would be indeed beautiful if it could fulfil all expectations. Everything here is on a grand scale; the breadth of the stream is from two to three hundred feet, the height of the fall eighty feet, and the mass of water is immense. Near the Falls stand two fine castles, and behind them rise the snow-covered Alps.

The view from Castle Laufen on the left bank is particularly grand. The formation of the rock on one side of the stream forces the shoot of water into the middle channel, thus forming a small space, between the rocks and the lower cascade. This space has been utilized for a construction of strong beams and cramp irons to enable travellers to approach closely the mighty Falls of the Rhine. Descending many steps from the castle to this bridge, and turning round the last rocky corner, this enormous mass of water is seldom seen without a feeling of horror. No work of human hands could resist this pressure even for a minute, if the direction of the stream were not already marked out by its upper course. Even the rocks shake perceptibly under the uninterrupted fall of this weight of several millions of pounds. The clear emerald green of the water changes into snow-white, foaming froth ; the seething waves, thundering down, heap themselves over the rocks which bar their course, and bury themselves in the sand of the river's bed, to reappear hissing and whirling further down. Clouds of spray ascend from this vortex, and the colours of the rainbow flash in calm purity over the ever-moving confusion of waters, " like love that watches madness."

Can you believe that anybody who could enjoy

this sight in nature could remain in a dark room
to see nothing but a picture of it? And yet, it
must be said that it is nature herself who is the
artist. Below the Falls the old tower-like castle
Wörth, now used as a place for refreshments,
stands in the middle of the stream. In one of its
upper rooms there is a board covered with white
linen, the windows are shut, and a "camera
obscura" quickly represents the whole of the
magnificent Falls of the Rhine with inimitable
exactness, giving every detail with charming correctness. This must be a valuable study for a
landscape painter; but even in this shape it would
still be difficult to reproduce. The charm is
broken by the first beam of light through the re-
opened window. I shall never forget the view I
had of the Falls. I was fortunate in seeing them
amply supplied with water, and in a bright sun, at
noon.

In the evening I arrived at Zürich, one of the
prettiest cities I have seen; it lies in a deep valley
just where the clear Limmat rushes from the lovely
lake. It is a splendid walk over the long bridge,
which crosses the river near the lake, and from

which a fine view of the town hall, the hall, and
the beautiful cathedral, can be obtained. At the
other end of the lake the snow-covered Alps of
Glarus, the St. Gothard, and the glaciers of the
Bernese Oberland towered up in a semicircle, and
were lit up by the sinking sun, while a bewitching
dusk was already resting on the smooth surface of
the lake, only slightly rippled by the passing of a
steamboat.

Zürich used to be fortified, and it is difficult to
believe that not nature but human hands have
built up these mountains of ramparts, which were
constructed to cut off the town from the surrounding heights. The pulling down of these
fortifications gives plenty of work. The building
ground at Zürich had risen to enormous prices,
and the streets were extremely narrow; but now
where the town is taking off her iron dress it
grows rapidly. There are some beautiful new
buildings, such as the Corn Market and the
Hospital. The proprietor of the excellent hotel
where I put up has bought a piece of the lake
for 12,000 florins. For the last three years he

has gone on filling it up, and he has already been offered 40,000 florins for this piece of building ground.

At Zürich I was pleased to read in the newspaper of the capture of Sayda in Syria with the remark : " The first in the ranks at the storming of the place were H.R.H. Archduke Albrecht and Captain Laue of the Prussian Army." If my friend had been a Frenchman, the whole grand nation would boast of it, but as he is only a Prussian, very likely nobody will take any notice of it.

To celebrate my birthday heaven favoured us with sunshine, which was quite a change, and I made a beautiful tour that I shall never forget ; from Zürich over the Albis, along the lake of Zug to Schwyz and Brunnen on the lake of Lucerne. The last few years I have spent this day in very different surroundings. In 1833 I was at Genoa, then at Copenhagen, then on the Bosphorus and on the Euphrates ; last year ill at Pesth, where I was so kindly nursed by my friend Vincke and his wife. This year I am hale and sound and happy at the foot of the Alps; and I did what I had never done before on October 28th,[1] namely, took a bath in the open air. You will see how much benefit I have derived from the treatment at Ilmenau, when I tell you that I bathed in the snow waters of the Rhine near Schaffhausen after having passed the night in a post-chaise, then in the clear waters of the Lake of Zürich, and to-day in the Lake of Lucerne, which was quite rough. The Föhn, a violent wind from the south, beat the waves like the billows of the sea on to the shore. I have left off wearing my cotton under-garments, and I am in excellent health this autumn, in spite of the cold rainy weather, but I must not boast.

Brunnen lies at the foot of the highest Alps. Beyond rises the Pilatus with its indented top and the Rigi, which, I am sorry to say, cannot be ascended this year, on account of the unusually early and heavy snow. At the sight of this mountain I thought of you, dear father, how your horse ran away with you as you were coming down; when

---

[1] Thus stated in the original letter; but, as is well known, his birthday was on October 26th. For similar mistake, see his journal written on his way to Constantinople ("Moltke: His Life and Character").

I saw the steepness of these rugged rocks, the thought of it was dreadful. Here at Brunnen the first Swiss alliance was made, and over at Grütli, in a little meadow, the second most important meeting was held; and where that simple little chapel stands on the steep mountain-side Tell sprang ashore, pushing back the governor's boat into the stormy lake. There may have been a gale on that day, such as we had on the 29th, but Gessler had no iron steamer like ours to fight against it. However, we had to cross the lake to Grütli in a rowing boat, violently tossed about before we could go aboard the steamer. The Föhn rushes so powerfully and irregularly out of the rocky valleys that the steamer had difficulty to reach Flüelen. The gusts of wind raised the surface of the water like a typhoon; we struggled against the elements, and progressed so slowly, that I had plenty of time to study the wonderful ramifications of the mountains.

From Altorf we made for St. Gothard; but now my story becomes rather exciting, and it is a pity that the fact of my writing this letter in Italy betrays to you that I have really crossed it. But the worst that can happen to a traveller on his tour happened to us: a sudden thaw and violent rain after heavy snows. As is well known, this route is much exposed to avalanches, especially numerous in winter and spring, of which, however, we were to have an example. After leaving Altorf the poor horses were hardly able to make way against the violent wind. In spite of drenching rain, I remained on the box of the *diligence*, to enjoy the grand scenery. I had never before seen such valleys, such walls of rock rapidly descending from a height of about a thousand feet, and such a turbulent stream as the Reuss. The high road wound higher along the declivity of the mountains, and the stream roared deeper under us in ghastly ravines. The rocks approached closer to each other, the road suddenly curved, and, crossing a bold arch, now went along the other side of the valley. Not far from the village of Vasen a thundering noise was suddenly heard through the loud roaring of the stream. Opposite us, high up near the snow-line, we saw a dark mass loosening and rolling down the ravine with ever-increasing rapidity. Its course was marked by a

cloud of vapour; it appeared to sight again farther
down, big stones and pieces of rock preceded it in
mad jumps, and with a dreadful crash this mass of
stones and rock moved down into the stream. We
were standing straight over it, but about two
hundred feet from the bottom of the valley, which
enabled us to gaze upon the spectacle without
danger. In a moment the bed of the Reuss was
completely dammed up, the swollen stream roared
and foamed, but the next minute it had overcome
the obstacle, and rushed along with a darkened
colour over fragments of rocks and trunks of trees.
Such a fall of stones is a small thing and only dangerous to those whom it overtakes; but what a
landslip means, I had seen the preceding day at
Goldau. There it happened, I think in 1806, that
a mountain-side slipped and buried in a few
minutes a populous village rich in cattle, fields,
and houses. Goldau is situated about a quarter,
perhaps half, a German mile from the top of that
mountain, and if I had not seen it, I should never
have believed it possible that blocks of stone of the
size of a house could roll on for such a distance.
But, once set in motion, nothing can stop them.

Even to-day the sight of the place is dreadful. For more than a mile in circumference stones are heaped upon stones ten to twenty feet high, so that scarcely a fir-tree grows in this scene of desolation, once the fertile pleasant home of man; it is a Herculaneum for coming centuries; under these masses of stones the customs of our times will be studied as we to-day study those of the Romans under the ashes of Vesuvius.

Before we reached the village of Göschenen, a mass of rocks and stones had slipped on to the road behind us; this with another in front of us, prevented our carriage from moving either onwards or backwards. Nothing was left for us but to walk on. This was by no means easy, for the spaces between the loose *débris* were filled up with mud, into which we sank up to our knees, in the darkness. To delay would have been dangerous as fragments continued to fall. In pitch dark and in pouring rain we arrived at Göschenen. Men were sent to fetch our baggage, and the horses were brought in, but the carriage will probably have to remain where it is for some time.

On the following day the wind had sunk a little,

but the rain came down all the more steadily. We did not, however, let it prevent us from continuing our wanderings, nor did it disturb our delight in the awful grandeur of the Alpine valley. Near the Schöllenen there are such dangerous places, that from time to time so-called *refuges* have been constructed ; they are niches cut in the rocks in which the traveller can hide when he sees an avalanche approaching, and they are frequent here. And by day this could easily be done. From the height of a thousand feet a stone would ordinarily fall in about eight seconds, along the rocky wall it would fall about three or four times as quickly. This would enable anyone to escape who took care to run about a hundred paces away in the right direction. During the night some stones had slipped down here, and it was very difficult to pass, on account of the swollen brook. Near the devil's bridge (Teufelsbrücke) the character of the valley is very wild. The high perpendicular granite walls on both sides, and the fall of the Reuss from the height of a hundred feet, under the arches of the bridge have often been described and represented. Then you enter Urner Loch, a

gallery hewn out of the solid rock, from whose
dark depths you suddenly see before you the spire
of the church at Andermatt and the Zwingthurm
near the village hospital standing out from a large
meadow.   The church is the oldest in Switzerland,
it was built in the year 600.

Everything here was covered with snow, and we
had to continue our journey on sledges of light
structure; empty barrels formed the seats, and
they were drawn by one horse.   Each traveller
had a sledge for himself.   There were three of us;
a Swiss alderman from Unterwalden, a Frenchman, and myself.   Three Germans, travelling
journeymen, who had enlisted in the Papal Army,
were pilgrimaging on foot to Rome.   About an
hour before Hospenthal the road was so completely blocked up by avalanches that the horses
could go no further.   We had provided ourselves
with three strong Swiss lads, who carried our luggage, so we walked and climbed.   Suddenly the
guide cried out " Una valanga," and at the same
moment we saw on the opposite side, about two
hundred feet behind us, a mass of snow rolling
down from the top.   It is almost incredible that

mere snow can cause such a terrific noise, and yet this avalanche, which was but small and hardly reached the brook, caused a noise like that of continuous thunder.

From this point the expedition began to be uncomfortable. The higher we ascended the softer became the snow, the result of rain and a south wind. We sank into it up to our knees, even to our waists. And often while endeavouring to extricate one leg we sank just as deeply with the other. For a while we could endure it, but after an hour's struggle the gale became more violent, rain and fog much denser, and we began seriously to long for the walls of the hospice, which, however, were not yet to be seen. I had given my mantle to one of the lads, and had nothing else to carry, so I reached it first, the Frenchman was about half-an-hour behind us, and the lads, already heavily laden, had to support him. At last our whole caravan arrived.

You can scarcely imagine a more miserable inn than that of the St. Gothard. The government of the canton Ticino has built a large house with many rooms, but the most necessary thing, stoves, have been forgotten. There is only one in the whole house, and this one was so draped with wet cloaks and trousers, that it gave no heat in any other part of the large room. Our luggage was wet through, and all we could do was to go to bed at five o'clock in the afternoon, after we had had some hot wine and macaroni with cheese. In the hospice proper there are only two Capuchin monks and a lay brother, who, with their scanty means, supply poor and needy travellers. They have none of those big dogs now, who used to find lost travellers.

On the following day we descended the south side of the pass; there was still more snow than on the north side. The road here winds along extremely steep mountains in endless zig-zags; we climbed straight down a path which, without the snow, even a chamois would not attempt. If we had not continually sunk in up to our hips, we should have broken our necks; we had numerous falls, but each time the snow saved us; and so we toiled for three hours in continual rain. Not till we arrived at Airolo, almost a thousand feet lower than on the north side, did the snow cease. But now it became very dangerous to climb down the steep, slippery grass. The wind caught my mantle, and together with a recruit of His Holiness, I sailed *vent en poupe*, down a green slope much quicker than I liked. We were landed happily on a snow-field. The Frenchman involuntarily followed our example, but head foremost, and he would have been thrown into an abyss, had not one of the guides, who was in advance, planted a snow shovel in his course and stopped him in this way. But the poor devil had damaged his knee so badly that he had to stay behind at Airolo.

This place we reached in three days, not having once taken off our wet clothes. There was no need for me to continue my baths.

We had hoped to pursue our journey from Airolo in a comfortable carriage, but we were disappointed. The Ticino, a dangerous mountain stream, swollen by the unusually heavy and incessant rains, had destroyed many of the bridges, and damaged the fine road, even washing it away in places. So we were obliged to make our way on foot as far as Faido.

But the journey down the Leventine valley was

extremely pleasant and interesting. This part of
the country might be called the home of waterfalls,
and for a friend of this branch of nature's beauty
no better way can be proposed than to follow the
course of the Ticino. Heavy clouds still hung over
the valley bordered by dark firs, but high above
them towered the snow-capped mountains, and now
and then specks of blue sky showed, seeming to
give promise of better times. We now reaped the
advantage of the heavy rains by seeing the water-
falls at their best. Hundreds and hundreds of
cascades rushed down the mountains, each one of
them would have been worth a long journey to
see. The greater number of them only exist in a
sudden thaw, such as we had. Now they appear
like silver threads falling down from the clouds on
to the high, dark rocks, then they roll down like a
glistening veil from rock to rock, soon they spring
like fountains over blocks of stone which bar
their way, or rush foaming madly down a deep
abyss of sixty or a hundred feet. The rapidity
of the falling water decreases, because it dissolves
into mist and sinks down in graceful foam.

The *Dazo grande* is a very imposing sight. The

Ticino, with its very rapid course, forms a current above Faido, which certainly falls three hundred feet in a distance of about five hundred. The stream runs through such a narrow ravine and between such high perpendicular and often projecting rocks, that the road had, in many places, to be cut into the solid stone, in others it had to be carefully built up with free-stone to the height of from thirty to forty feet. The water seems not to find sufficient room in the bed of the river; in two places the stream is only two feet wide, while in its upper course it has a width of fifty or a hundred feet; if it were possible to get down to these narrow places, they could easily be stepped over. The river bed must either enlarge underneath the surface of the water or it must be immensely deep. With terrific force the pent-up water rushes out of these crevices into the larger basins, tumbling in seething foam over the rocks, thundering from fall to fall, while the winding road endeavours to follow its course. Insensibly one leaves the fir-tree behind for the chestnut, the walnut, the vine, cypress and the olive.

The first sight of Bellinzona is peculiar. Three forts forming a long wall and reaching as far as the bridge over the Ticino, which is 250 feet long, shut off the valley, two thousand feet wide, from the high mountains on the left hand. The wall is constructed so that it is a defence on both sides, and the little town itself is fortified.

I have had time to write this long letter, as the steamer is not crossing the lake to-day on account of the bad weather. It is no use going to Italy in such weather as this, we might as well be at the Christmas Fair in Berlin. It rains incessantly, the water of Lago Maggiore has risen fourteen feet. Our hotel is on an island, and one cannot leave the house. In the yard, where we walked about yesterday, boats are required to-day.

Naples, Nov. 17th, 1840.

Now I have exchanged the bleak mountains of the Thuringian Forest for the shores of the Gulf of Naples, the dark firs whose branches sunk under the weight of the snow for the light green of the lemon tree with its golden fruit, and the olive and

the palm. Through the open door of my balcony
I see, on the opposite shore, Vesuvius with thick,
white clouds rising from its crater. Vineyards and
gardens cover its base, and an uninterrupted row of
houses and palaces—the villages of Portici, Torre
del Annunciata, Torre del Greco, and Castellamare
—extends along the shore. A little further on
the right the promontory of Sorrento juts into the
sea, and the island of Capri raises its rugged head
out of the water; close under my windows I hear
the continuous bustle of this populous city. Everything here is noisy, even the dashing of the sea
against the rocky shore, and the quays seem noisier
to me than in other places. The oyster and fish
sellers with their " Frutti di Mare," the donkey-
boys, who bring immense loads of vegetables,
which at home are only seen in the early summer, flower and grape sellers, coachmen, beggars,
and even sluggards shout, if they do nothing else.
If a " lazzarone " feels bored he yells, and immediately a crowd assembles round him who also
yell to keep him company, and suddenly they all
seem satisfied. There you see two fellows playing
" a la mora," a game in which you guess how

many fingers your partner will raise; by the noise
they make you would think they were coming to
blows, but they are only conversing in a friendly
way. Further on, people are playing with mud
balls " il bigliardo del povero," but all this is
done with loud screaming. The horses wear bells,
and since every one exerts his lungs to the utmost,
it is most difficult to make oneself heard. A
kind of stupefaction comes over you as you walk
through these noisy streets; suddenly a cab drives
close up to you, " Volete carrozza ! " calls out the
driver, as loud as ever he can, and he obliges
you to make a round to get out of his way.
" Eccellenza ! " cries another, and points with a re-
proving glance at your boots, which have become
very bespattered in the dirty street, and while you
are looking at them, the man has already seized
you by the leg. He puts a little foot-stool under
your foot and in the midst of the crowd of people
and horses he restores the polish of your " chaus-
sure" for two grani. "Andiamo alla barca ! "
shouts a little sailor, barring your way. " Per
carità, Signore ! " calls a beggar, stretching out his
crutch, so that you are obliged to get over it. On

all sides you are detained by people trying to make you give them some trifle. A German beggar opens the door for you, an Italian shuts it —both for the sake of a coin.

But before telling you more about Naples, I must give you a description of my journey here. I came by water and in water. Dreadful rains had swelled the rivers in the north of Italy, so as to interrupt all communication. The large boat-bridge over the Po was torn away, we had to em-bark, with our wet baggage in little boats, and thus in some danger to cross the wild stream. The weather was horrible, and I hastened to leave a country already known to me, in search of new sights. Everything was seen at a disadvantage. The Borromean Islands in the Lago Maggiore were not much more beautiful than the *Möven Island* in the *Schlei*, and even *Genova la superba* was not nearly so magnificent as usual.

But this Queen of the Sea will for ever tell of the time when kingdoms were her subjects. The palaces of Durazzo, Balbi, Doria, Caretto, Lavagna, and many others are of royal magnificence. The most costly thing in Genoa, that is space, is lavished on them. If you would see beautiful staircases, you must come here. The steps are often as wide as fifty feet, they are mostly of white and black marble, ornamented with precious statues on both sides and ascend very gently. They lead up to the first and second storeys, where there is nothing to be seen till you reach the dwelling apartments. You have to climb high to get away from the darkness of the narrow streets, but then you are rewarded by a magnificent view. The streets, Balbi nuova and nuovissima are wide, and magnificently paved with large square stones, but near the harbour the streets are often very narrow, no wider than a path. My rooms at the *Croce di Malta* were a hundred and twenty steps high. The dining-room occupied two storeys, and was more like a church than a hall. Stepping out on to the flat roof of the house, you are surprised to find yourself in a lovely orange grove with a bubbling fountain. The water is laid on from the mountains, which rise close behind Genoa, to the height of three thousand feet ; they are covered with country houses, gardens, olive plantations. The forts which crown these hills make Genoa a *reduit* for the whole army of the kingdom.

The magnificent sight of Palazzo Lavagna recalled to me vividly Schiller's Fiesco, and the paroxysm of ambition which seizes him when, opening the large doors of his room, he beholds Genoa before him in the splendour of the rising sun. Quite at the opposite end lies Palazzo Doria, the home of Andreas Doria, whose descendants are still flourishing, while the house of Lavagna became extinct with " the Lion."

Though the sight of the Mediterranean was beautiful as the waves beat against the rocky shore, the tossing became most disagreeable as soon as our steamer *Sully* passed the point of the Molo. The night was dark and stormy and all the passengers were ill. One of them, who was sleeping on deck, was most unfortunate, a yard fell down and broke his skull ; the poor man, a Russian, barely escaped with his life. It was a long passage ; when we were already in sight of Leghorn the storm became so violent, that we began to think of turning back. However, towards evening we reached the roadstead (we ought to have been there in the morning), and entered the harbour. The captain decided to stay twenty-four hours to let the gale subside.

Every traveller at sea makes the acquaintance of a gale as a " matter of course," and I leave it to you to deduct from my description as much as you think necessary. But the fact remains that I was horribly sea-sick, and that I almost made up my mind never to go on board a ship again. The following day the sky was blue, the air mild, the sea bright, the ship began to get up steam, the anchor was weighed, and we were out at sea again. But during the night the " sirocco " rose ; our misery began again and continued till we sailed into the " molo " of Civita Vecchia. Now I had had enough. I disembarked, intending to go to Rome, and from there to Naples ; but our passes had to be *viséd*. I was sent from the Police-station to the Douane, from the Prussian Consul to the Papal Legate, from the Post-office to the Custom-house ; everywhere I had to pay, and matters were nowhere satisfactorily settled. No city has ever impressed me so unfavourably as this one. Swarms of ragged beggars crowded round me, every one of them seized a piece of my luggage, running away with my travelling bag, my umbrella, or my mantle. At last, when all the difficulties were overcome, I was asked to pay for two places in the *diligence*, because otherwise it could not leave till the next morning. They seemed to make sure of me, perhaps they could tell by my face that I did not like a boisterous sea ; but I made up my mind quickly, took a boat, had my luggage put in and embarked again on the *Sully*, which went rocking on slowly in the direction of Cape Circello. If the companions of Ulysses had been as sick as I and my fellow-sufferers, there would have been no need for them to stop their ears with wax. No sirens could have succeeded in making us listen to their beautiful songs.

At Civita Vecchia, which looks beautiful from the sea, I was so happy as to make the acquaintance of the most notorious robber-chieftain of our times. He had led many expeditions, on which no less than thirty men had been murdered at one time, and in spite of all his crimes he seemed well pleased with himself. At last a treaty had been made between His Holiness and Signor Gasparino in consequence of which the latter had been sent to Ancona. But not very long after, this *bravo* thinking that he had been taken advantage of, re-

D

fused to keep the contract. He again headed his
band and plundered worse than before. The
Papal Government made a new treaty with him.
The robber captain was given comfortable apartments at Civita Vecchia ; he now receives four paoli
per day and four courses at his meals, and leads a
quiet life under the care of a guard. He was, at
any rate, the most amiable person I met at Civita
Vecchia.

I am sure that travelling long in Italy must
deteriorate the character. The Italians seem to
be a nation of Facchini, Camerieri, Vetturini,
Hospiti and Ciceroni, who have united to
plunder the traveller. It is true they cheat him
to gain but a trifle, but it is always vexing to be
taken in. The consequence is that bad intentions are often suspected, even where they do
not exist. Nobody can be trusted ; for every
purchase one has to bargain, and yet one is
cheated every time. In Germany, if the poor
man expects a reward for rendering you a service,
in Italy the beggar forces you to give him
something ; making himself as unbearable as
possible that you may rid yourself of him by

giving him an alms. He holds you by your coat, shows you the most nauseous wounds and mutilations, abuses you if you don't give him what he asks for, and laughs at you when you do. If you ask the name of the street, your informant stretches out his hand for a reward. A decently clad man followed me through Leghorn to show me the Prussian Consul's house which had already been pointed out to me. I told him that he need not trouble himself, as I should not give him anything. " Ecco la casa, al terzo piano " (on the third floor) said the man and went away. Astonished at his modesty, I ascended the high stairs, and found that the consul lived on the ground floor.

It is best not to give an Italian all that you intend to give him at once. If he receives five francs for ever so small a service he is sure to say : " è poco, Signor" (it is little). But supposing you gave him first one franc then half a franc, he would very likely be satisfied. This is a low trait in his character. Satisfied with anything if necessary, he will try to get more as long as there is a possibility.

On the 10th of November, at noon, we were under the shelter of the Island of Ischia. We passed quickly by the high castle of Procida, and the beautifully shaped Cape Miseno, sailed through the bay of Baja and Puzzuoli, rounded the Posilippo, and beautiful Naples lay before us. But clouds hung about Vesuvius and darkened Cape Sorrento, diminishing the beauty of the view that we had expected to enjoy. I saw Constantinople for the first time, at the end of November, and I must say that in beauty it exceeds Naples.

The chamberlain von Oertzen, whose acquaintance I made on the journey, and I, have taken comfortable and cheap apartments together on the Strada Lucia, whence I make my excursions.

One of the most interesting objects to be seen in Italy is Pompeii. You are transported, as if by magic, from the present into past ages, from the nineteenth century into the first century of the Christian era. Time, migration of nations, and amateurs in art, have destroyed the most magnificent, most solid constructions of the Greeks and Romans. Nothing is left of the gigantic temples and theatres, but isolated shafts of columns, and half-sunken vaults. But Pompeii was overwhelmed by a convulsion of nature, and in one day, in the midst of life her inhabitants were caught, *en flagrant délit*, and entombed for two thousand years.

The earth itself was the museum that preserved not only the works of art, but all the household arrangements of the population. A layer of ashes and pumice-stone, ten to twenty feet thick, protected all these things from destruction; at the beginning of the last century it was known that Pompeii had been buried by an eruption of Vesuvius in the year A.D. 79, but not where the city was situated. Some inscriptions found in well-sinking gave the first indication of the site. At present about a fourth, perhaps the most interesting, part of the old town, with its vineyards and country-houses, has been brought to light. The following buildings have been excavated: the forum, two theatres, the street of the artisans and merchants, the amphitheatre before the gates, the street of tombs, and the houses of some well-known men, such as Cicero, Diomedes, Sallust, etc.

At the time of the eruption the inhabitants of Pompeii were assembled at the amphitheatre, whose marble steps and lions' cages are now spread out before our eyes. Very likely most of them had time to save themselves; yet many bodies have been found of those who were overtaken. Before the door of the large beautiful house of the freedman Diomedes, the skeleton of a man was found with a key in one bony hand, and a bag of money in the other.

In the lower vaults of the temple of Isis lay the skeleton of another with a crowbar in his hand; the man had worked himself through two thick walls. A woman's skeleton was found with two children in her arms, whom she must have tried to protect from the rain of ashes; a petrified piece of ashes is still shown to the travellers, with the impression of a beautiful bosom.

But nothing is more surprising in visiting this Epimenides of towns, than the freshness of the colours, which have covered the walls for about two thousand years. Almost all the floors of the bigger houses are inlaid with most delicate mosaics, and the fountains, ornamented with fragile cockles

and shells, look as if they had only just been
finished. You would marvel at the correctness
of the drawing and the brightness of the colours
of the floating figures, on red and black back-
grounds, which adorn the walls, having reference to
the different purposes of the several rooms. One
pillar, found in the house of a cloth manufacturer,
explains the whole process of this business; there
are the loom, the damping and washing machines,
and also a press worked with screws in the same
manner as those of the present day. The dining-
rooms are decorated with paintings of fruit, flowers
and hunting scenes. The names of the artisans as
well as those of the streets, are written on the houses
in good writing and generally in red; sometimes
there are witty mottoes and figures painted in
much the same way as they are found on our
walls. The carriage wheels have left their marks
in the hard lava pavement, and in some places the
stones, put for crossing the street in wet weather,
are still lying there. Bread, flour, olives, figs,
beans have been found (all charcoaled), wine,
jugs (pointed amphoras as they are used to-day in
the East), numerous potter's vessels of most dainty

shape with well-known figures on black ground, stoves, ovens, all kinds of tools, surgical and musical instruments, dice, chess-boards, kitchen utensils and scales, and all these things only differ from our present fashions in that they are more highly finished and in better taste.

Considering that Pompeii was only a country-town of secondary importance, it is astonishing to see the number of bronze and marble statues, of paintings and mosaics, of vases and jewellery, which have been dug out. The *Forum civile* must have been very beautiful; it is a square place arranged according to the proportions of Vitruvius. The summit of the hill of Castella-mare and the crater of Vesuvius, which brought this ruin upon the town, can be seen from here. On three sides of it there are more than two thousand Doric columns in good preservation. They are of tuffa covered with stucco and painted red or yellow. These columns used to form a portico, or covered walk, but the beautifully carved cornices have fallen in. On the fourth side stood a temple where was found the gigantic head of a Jupiter. Twelve magnificently grooved marble

pillars of the peristyle are still standing. The
Curia, the *Basilica*, the *Temples of Mercury* and
Concordia, the *Pantheon* come next. The many
statues which adorned this square have been taken
to the museum at Naples, as well as the greater
part of the art treasures, paintings and mosaics.
If they had been left in their old places they would
probably have been soon destroyed. But it is to
be regretted that not one Roman house has been
restored here, where all necessary material was at
hand.

The ancients bestowed much more trouble and
expense on their public buildings and less on their
own houses than we, but everything was neat
even to the veriest detail. The rooms which surrounded a square court-yard are seldom larger
than eight to ten feet square ; they are unconnected
with one another.

The Pompeians must have had frequent intercourse with the Egyptians. This is proved by
their sculptures, papyri, their temple of Isis and
the mummies that have been found. If one of
these could rise and take a look at us, he would
be as much surprised at our appearance in coats

and round hats, and at our arrival by train, as we are at his town.

At a chemist's medicine bottles of glass containing medicines, and marble jugs, with balsams for the embalming of mummies, were found. I have been lucky enough to obtain a little piece of this hard mass which, in spite of the two thousand years that have elapsed, still retains a strong smell.

AUGUSTE VON MOLTKE.

SELECTIONS FROM LETTERS TO HIS
SISTER AUGUSTE.

AUGUSTE VON MOLTKE, the youngest sister of the Field-Marshal,
was born at Augustenhof in Holstein, on September 16th,
1809. From her earliest childhood she had always been her
brother's favourite, and very early the rich endowments of her
character were seen in her humility, kindness of heart, and
ready self-denial. On the 21st of May, 1834, she was married
to John Heyliger Burt, of Colton, near Lichfield in England,
owner of the plantation of St. John on the island of St. Croix
in the West Indies. Her husband, who had lived in Germany
for some time, had by his first wife, Ernestine von Staffeldt,
three children, the youngest of whom, Marie, afterwards became
the wife of the Field-Marshal. How much devotion Auguste

von Moltke lavished on the education of her step-children, and
with what affection they returned her care has been told in
the biography of " Marie Moltke." (See " Moltke : His Life
and Character.")

The Burts lived first at Schleswig, then at Itzehoe ; their
marriage was a very happy one ; Auguste presented her husband
with two children, a son, Henry, later aide-de-camp of the Field-
Marshal, and a daughter, Ernestine. In 1855, Mr. Burt
determined to go and see his property in the West Indies ;
on his way home he was taken ill and died on board on the
25th of July, 1856 ; his body was buried at sea. In 1864, when
her brother Fritz lost his wife, Auguste (though still mourning
for her husband) went to him to comfort him in his trouble.
She remained with him, took the cares of the household upon
herself, and made his lonely life bright again. In December
of the year 1868, when Marie, the Field-Marshal's wife, fell
ill, she hastened to the sick-bed of the dear daughter, but her
faithful and self-sacrificing care did not succeed in keeping off
the dreaded evil ; Marie died on the evening of Christmas
Day. Auguste now resolved to devote herself to her brother
Helmuth, who was severely shaken by the loss of his beloved
wife. And she was encouraged in her determination by the
gracious words of Queen Augusta, who gave her an audience
at which she told her that it was her duty to remain with her
brother, who must be preserved for his King and his Fatherland.
She and her brother Fritz then went to live with the Field-
Marshal, over whose households in Berlin and at Creisau she
henceforth presided. On March 27th, 1883, death ended her
useful life, which was full of blessing to others and whose
motto had been : "Rejoicing in hope, patient in tribulation,
continuing instant in prayer." How much her brother Helmuth
must have loved her is shown by the fact that he buried her
remains in the vault at Creisau, where he now rests himself
between his wife and his favourite sister.

Charput, July 4th, 1838.[1]

MY DEAR SISTER GUSTCHEN,

Your welcome letter of April 12th has
found its way to Armenia safely. I received it on
our march here, and as we have been resting for
three days I will not delay any longer, but answer
it in spite of my planned laziness. Having been
for two months in continual movement, sleeping
either in a tent or in the open air, I can say with
Falstaff, "Wenn ich weiss, wie das Innere eines
'Zimmers' aussieht, bin ich ein Brauerpferd, ein
Bündel Radies."[2] Just now I am stretched out
on cushions in a good, high apartment; I am lazy
à dessein, and do not stir a finger unless obliged,
eat after well considering my digestion, avoiding
Turkish favourite dishes as "pillav" with honey
and cream, sour milk with cut-up cucumbers and
garlic, &c. A case of champagne has fortunately
arrived for me, and I hope that I and my exhausted

---

[1] *Compare* Letter No. 48 in "Briefe über Zustände und
Begebenheiten in der Türkei," p. 284 (5th Edition).

[2] "Henry IV.," act iii. scene 3 : "And I have not forgotten
what the inside of a church is made of, I am a peppercorn, a
brewer's horse."

horses will be in good condition again in a few days.

This time I write my letter to you, my dear Gustchen, partly to answer your kind letter and also because father will probably not have returned from his journey when it arrives. But I shall not forget to drink his health on the 12th of this month in a bottle of French sherbet.

Really I have nothing more to tell you than that we crossed the Anti-Taurus by a perilous path, and then leisurely descended the Euphrates, which is only four hours distant from our present headquarters.

After the revolts of the Kurds in the Karsan mountains (the most precipitous that can be imagined) had been put down, I went with the Commander to their camp on the foot of the hills where they had left their tents and luggage. The temperature here was about ten degrees warmer than amongst the snowy summits. There were no fine walnut-trees to give shade, no rustling mountain brooks, and the life in the tents, which we could hardly leave during the day on account of the heat, was made very disagreeable at night by

quantities of scorpions, tarantulæ and 'snakes
which we killed every day, but of which we never
got rid altogether.   However, none of them belonged to the most virulent species, the only
danger was in being stung by them.   But millions
of most insufferable flies did not allow us a minute's
rest as long as it was day-light.   I should have
been thankful for one of your veils.   But one
thing I can say in favour of this country, there are
no bugs, and this circumstance makes up, in my
opinion, for all the other plagues of insects.

We were heartily pleased when Hafiz Pasha
declared at supper, on the 25th of June, that we
should break up in an hour.   He intended to visit
a place in the Taurus where new iron works were
to be constructed, and wished to precede the
troops.   Though we were without military escort,
except some cavasses with long lances, our procession numbered almost two hundred horse.
Each horseman carried his own arms, and most of
them had guns over their shoulders.

In brilliant moonlight we passed through a
wide and fertile but uncultivated plain, without
dwelling-places, a real desert; for no Kurd dares to

settle where the fruits of his industry are not protected by high mountains.

After a two hours' ride we heard the roaring of the Battman stream, and soon found ourselves confronted by a wonderful construction, a bridge of formidable height which spans in a single arch, with a tension of a hundred feet, the wild impetuous mountain stream. This bridge probably dates from the time when the Genoese constructed works here to protect their Indian trade. Neither the industry nor the diligence of the Turks has been able to destroy them completely during the space of two hundred years. Other monuments of this small, far-away, though important commercial town are seen in the strong castle and two bridges over the Tigris at Djesireh, destroyed by Reschid Pasha only two years ago, and a bridge over the stream at Hösn-Keifa built in the same bold style of architecture, but now fallen in. Then their trade route seems to have gone towards the north along the Battman over the Taurus and the Murad down to Palu, where on an isolated rock of about two thousand feet rise the ruins of one of their castles, a position almost unassailable. The strong castles on the summits of the heights at Tokat, Turchal, and Amasia, must have been built by the Genoese on foundations of much older date, they seem to have been connected with the fortified sea-side places of Samsoon and Sinope.

We then rode along the foot of the mountains, till, towards morning, we arrived at the town of Farkin or rather at an extensive ruin, between whose old pillars and arches detached mud huts are built. Meya-Farkin must once have been an important town. Walls of large and carefully hewn stones are, for the greater part, still preserved. Their construction is exactly similar to that of Diarbekir, only that at Farkin sandstone is used, while Diarbekir is built of basalt. Within the walls are beautiful remains of churches and houses, but they are only ruins, as for hundreds of years much has been destroyed and nothing restored in this land. Our only resting place was a damp field, where we stayed whilst our horses grazed for a few hours.

Though we had been in the saddle for ten hours, we continued our journey the following morning,

and rode for six more hours, with the same horses—
our own good horses—and that when they had no
oats to eat, but only grass.   At noon we turned to
the right, ascending a narrow valley, to the pretty
town of Hasru.   The surrounding mountains have
greatly protected cultivation.   A beautiful clear
mountain stream, plantations of poplars, whose
slim trunks rise up close to one another like the
blades of a corn-field, large walnut and mulberry
trees and extensive vineyards, give a most friendly
appearance to the place.   A tent was put up for
the Pasha, on the flat roof of the Musselim's house,
from which we had a lovely view over the mountains and the plain, and then we had our much-
needed dinner.

Here, as everywhere, the Pasha received peti-
tions and complaints from the inhabitants and
checked many abuses.   But as long as the evil is
not attacked at the root, such help can only be
incomplete.

The next morning we climbed a height only to
descend on the other side down a path cut in steps.
I think only native horses with circular shoes could
do such a journey without being lamed.   Towards

evening we reached Illidsha, another pleasantly situated little mountain town. We entered with the Pasha a beautiful, vaulted hall where a fountain was playing; and we did not object to some sherbet and pipes, which were offered to us, nor did we object to being perfumed with aloë and sprinkled with rose-water.

After another troublesome ride, we arrived towards evening at Sivan-Maaden, a desolate mountain-valley where a foundry is to be built. Some of the horses could not keep up; the poor animals had been without food for fourteen hours, so we halted for a day.

The valleys and slopes of this mountain-range are covered with big and small black stones or lumps of iron ore; the richness of the ore is so great that it contains more than fifty per cent. of pure iron. In our country iron has often to be brought up from a depth of a thousand feet, with great trouble, but here it has only to be picked up; there is enough to last about a hundred years. The same abundance is found in a mountain-stream not far off; this rivulet joins the Tigris, and with the help of blasting, it could be made navigable.

A Frenchman of the name of Chatillon had been sent here to construct a furnace, and we were just in time to save him from the intrigues of Turkish officials. The work, which had made no progress at first, is now carried on with great zeal by the help of the Pasha.

We also brought help to a German countryman, an honest and skilful blacksmith. In the presence of the Pasha he made out of iron which he had smelted himself, a very good steel sword, for which the Pasha rewarded him generously. The Pasha gave a beautiful horse to M. Chatillon, promised to decorate him with the Nishan, if he were successful, and granted him, what was more valuable than anything else, protection against the ignorance and malice of the proper authorities.

The following morning a two hours' ride brought us to the banks of the Murad, a south tributary of the Euphrates, which rushes along here through mountains that up to July are covered with snow. These mountains must be about 12,000 or 13,000 feet above the level of the sea. As you, my dear Guste, are not the sole reader of my letters, you must not mind if I make a geographical note here.

It is very remarkable that the tributaries of the Tigris spring in the immediate neighbourhood of the shores of the Murad, which even in summer is here a river the size of the Moselle. The springs of two of these rivulets are separated from the Murad at most about a thousand paces, and by a slight elevation, breaking through the snow-capped mountains, they only unite with the waters to which they were once so near, after a course of about three hundred hours.

The Pasha, a khan who was driven away from Daghestan, the Zeni of the camp, Mühlbach and myself as well as some servants embarked now on a raft of sheep-skin. To protect ourselves from the scorching sunbeams we made a roof of branches, and so we descended the rapid stream after our long, fatiguing journey. Mighty heights rose on both sides. Cheerful villages were seen in the shade of the beautiful large trees in the valleys. The inhabitants plunged into the sea-green whirlpools of the stream, in order to get for us apricots and mulberries, which are very fine and sweet here. A rocky wall on the left, seven or eight hundred feet high, was particularly beautiful. In some places the whirlpools were very violent, our "kelek" or raft shot along like an arrow, and the waves, beating on the rocks, came back foaming over our deck. No boat, not even a wooden raft, could pass these places, but the sheep-skins tied together by thin wicker-work, flexible like a fish, bend with the waves and rise on the surface like a feather; unless they are swamped, as we were at Djesirch, where the pillars of the bridge formed a kind of funnel six or eight feet deep. This time we reached Palu, of whose high tower I have told you before, without any accident. We now toiled up the steep and dirty streets of the town, and we were rewarded by excellent quarters at the house of a rich and most hospitable Armenian banker. Our horses arrived late in the evening. At last we reached Charput on the following day, when we did our best to recoup our strength in every way. But in a few days we shall, very likely, make a fresh start and go to Malatia.

H. M.

Trouville-sur-mer,
Department Calvados,
September 30th, 1850.

Dear Guste,

I am afraid you will think us quite lost, and I hasten to tell you that we are well and that we have already taken half-a-dozen sea-baths, which have been beneficial.

Marie sent you our last news from Rehme. It had begun to be quite winterly there, when we left on the 7th inst. We stayed a few days at Koblentz where we saw many old friends; this was a great change after our life at Magdeburg. We went by steamer to Frankfort-on-the-Maine, admiring the beautiful banks of the Rhine, then by train through the lovely country of the Palatinate to Metz, a beautiful old city with a magnificent cathedral and French fortifications. But the monotonous French chalk plateau begins here with the dull country of Champagne, and this monotony is uninterrupted till you reach Soissons, where the country begins to be pleasant and the railway takes you along by the Marne to Paris in a few hours.

We remained a week there, favoured with most beautiful weather, that we might have time to see the principal sights of this immense capital. Our hotel was situated on the boulevards at one of the most interesting points of the city. After an early cup of coffee we used to set off, and did not return till evening, much fatigued by the pleasures of the day. In the mornings we looked about the town, we saw the Tuileries, Champs Elysées, Notre Dame, Jardin des plantes, and the shops which, rivalling each other in magnificence, occupy the ground-floors in almost all the streets. It is astonishing what a variety of things is offered for sale, and how tastefully, not only silks and caps and bonnets, but also eatables, fish, game, cheese, and fruit, are arranged. It is marvellous whence the purchasers of all these delicacies come, all the more so as everything is expensive.

The distances are so great that one cannot count upon having one's meals at home. But meals are served everywhere. The dinners à la carte are excellent, but the prices are very high. We kept your birthday at the celebrated " Very " in the

Palais Royal (now National) with a *déjeûner* and good champagne.

In the afternoons we used to take the train to Versailles, St. Cloud, Meudon, St. Denis, etc., and were generally favoured with fine weather. We dined at six o'clock and went to the opera or theatre at eight. We have been at the Variétés, where five pieces are performed one after the other, the Théâtre Français and the Opera.

As the season was advancing we had to think seriously of our intended sea-baths. The railway from Paris to Havre by Rouen runs through a beautiful country in the lovely Seine valley. Many bridges cross over the winding river, and viaducts, a hundred feet high, are built over the valleys. After crossing one of these viaducts the train rushes with tremendous rapidity towards a steep chalk wall; it seems as if it must be wrecked, when suddenly, entering a long tunnel of about two thousand paces, it emerges upon an entirely different country. Rouen, the capital of the old Normans, those bold Norwegian pirates who conquered England, Sicily, and Naples, and carried their banners even as far as the gates of

Jerusalem, is one of the finest cities of the world. The cathedral and the "Palais de justice" are beautiful buildings, far surpassing those of Notre Dame and St. Denis.

We found the sea-baths at Havre uninviting, and decided to cross the mouth of the Seine, which is about the width of two German miles, to come to Trouville, a charming little town with a lovely beach for bathing. On both sides rise the chalk cliffs of Normandy, covered with fine forests, and crowned with beautiful châteaux. A little river with wide green meadows on both banks is used as harbour, where day by day the oyster-fishers go out to sea, bringing home excellent soles, turbots, large rusty dabs with their long tails and all kinds of tasty sea-monsters, whose names I do not know in German.

Our room looks out on to the boundless sea, and only on the right rises the promontory of Havre, with its lighthouses. Large steamers are to be seen along the horizon, and in every direction fishing boats are crossing the water, whose high waves, at the present moment, are beating with tremendous roaring against the shore. A fresh north-westerly wind is blowing. Rapidly moving clouds come down now and then in heavy showers, and it requires some strength of mind to bathe in the sea, especially after the warm baths at Rehme. But this bathing is much more invigorating. As long as the tide permits, we shall bathe at ten o'clock; at half-past ten we have *déjeûner*, an excellent meal. We have hired horses and are now able to make excursions into the country. Dinner is served at half-past five o'clock, with many different courses, each one excelling the other, and in addition we have excellent appetites, which enable us to appreciate the good things. Life in this place is not expensive; and so we have decided to continue our baths here as long as ever the weather permits, and then to make a short trip to England, going by Dieppe and Boulogne.

I hope all is going well with you.

Helmuth.

Wildbad, October 4th, 1868.

Dear Guste,

It is time to give you news of us at last, as half of our time here has already passed.

We are rather late this year, most of the visitors are already leaving. The few that are left are chiefly invalids, many of them suffering from paralysis. It rains almost every day in this hill country, but when the sun breaks through the clouds, it is very beautiful in the narrow wooded valley of the Enz. Here, as everywhere in the Black Forest, thick fir-woods cover the hills and at their feet are meadows of a lovely fresh green. Well-kept paths lead up to the hills in all directions.

The baths are beautiful and quite unique. They are made of china, the natural granite forming the bottom of the bath, which is carefully covered with sand to protect the feet. Immediately out of the rock gushes the warm spring, twenty-seven and a half degrees R. which supplies the baths with water of the same temperature without any interruption.

This water is similar to the springs at Gastein and Ragatz. Chemical analysis has not discovered any other constituents in it but those of distilled water, and the effect seems to be based upon the natural warmth of the earth, upon magnetic or electric power, two agents with which science is at present but imperfectly acquainted. At first the baths made me very tired, and I suffered again from palpitations of the heart, as I did thirty years ago. But now they agree well with me. The physicians tell me that the baths stir up all old complaints, but that they also cure them. To tell you the truth, I think that six weeks at Creisau will do me more good than at any watering-place.

Marie has taken ten baths, and is in excellent health.

The food is very good here, and we have every comfort. The North German Postal Union is delightful; I can send my letter from the Black Forest to Lubeck for one gr. (one penny), a distance of 150 German miles.

I cannot get Marie away from her book about horse-breeding, therefore I can only send her love to you and Fritz to-day.

Most affectionately,

HELMUTH.

Berlin, December 10th, 1868.

DEAR GUSTE,

Marie has fallen seriously ill; it seems to be

rheumatic fever.   It began with very violent pains
in her right foot, then in her left, and now it has
seized the whole of the left side, so that she can
only move her right arm.   The excessive pain has
decreased, but she is not able to move without
assistance.

The illness is a dangerous one, and Mr. Pesch
tells us it will last six weeks.   God grant that the
next, the most dangerous days, may be safely
passed.   Marie has had some sleep with the help
of morphia.

I have put off our Christmas guests, engaged a
nurse, and of course, everything that can possibly
relieve poor Marie's pains will be done.

It would be a great comfort, dear Guste, to have
you here, but I can scarcely expect you to come.

I shall write again as soon as a change for the
better or the worse occurs.

HELMUTH.

P.S. It seems to me as if Marie were better to-
day.   A mustard-plaster seems to give her relief.
She has a little appetite, and the fever is not so
high.   Three o'clock in the afternoon.

Berlin, January 4th, 1869.
7.30 a.m.

DEAR GUSTE,

I am very vexed with my second aide-de-camp for not having called me. I woke up early, but when I had lit my candle, I saw that it was only half-past three o'clock; I lay down again, half dressed, and did not wake up till I heard the carriage drive through the gateway. I should have liked so much to tell you again, how thankful I am for your devotion and self-sacrifice in nursing my poor Marie, and what a comfort you were to me, during the first sad days after her death. Such kindness is only to be repaid by gratitude and love, but misfortune must soften the hard crust of human hearts to bring them closer together. And how much kind sympathy I have received from all my other relations; may God reward you all.

It is a great comfort to me that Henry is coming, nothing could be more welcome to me, and I will write to-day to thank the good King for his delicate attentions. I should not like to detain dear Jeannette here more than a few days

longer.   She will be much missed at Segeberg,
and with Henry here I shall get on.

I cherish the hope that we shall all spend the
summer together quietly where we still have to
lay our dear departed for her last rest.   I hope
to receive the plan for the chapel to-day, and shall
then give orders for its building at once.

With best love and deep gratitude,

Your brother,

HELMUTH.

Meaux, September 16th, 1870.

DEAR GUSTE,

My best greetings and hearty congratulations for your birthday; want of time prevents
me from collecting my thoughts enough to write
a long letter.   My mind is continually dwelling
on our one aim, and in spite of all our success
I am weighed down by the cares of one day after
another.   The responsibility is too great, and the
continual strain most trying.

Your letters and Fritz's, which I receive from
time to time from our quiet home, are very
refreshing, but you also are too nearly concerned

to be able to enjoy it. Up to now God has graciously protected our people in the midst of dreadful losses and deaths. I feel rather exhausted, but I am fortunate in sleeping soundly, which always refreshes me again.

We have fine weather at last, but only nine or ten R. degrees of warmth, and without a fire the north rooms in the Palace of the Bishop of Meaux would be unbearable. I suppose it is not any warmer with you. If we had but come to the end of this. I hope for an early peace before the renewal of this blood-shedding. The boasting of the Paris authorities only shows their weakness. Much must be soon decided.

With heartiest greetings,

HELMUTH.

Versailles, December 20th, 1870.

DEAR GUSTE,

As this time of the year comes round and I remember our beloved Marie's sufferings, I often think with true thankfulness of the self-sacrificing care that you lavished upon her. I think it was

F

on this very day, two years ago, after having watched with her the whole night, that you called me in the morning with the joyful news that Marie was sleeping quietly. But our reviving hopes were not to be fulfilled. God had willed otherwise, and so it will be best. He has taken her to Himself in the prime of life, strength, and beauty, and spared her all the hardships of old age. It is a great comfort to me that all your letters, for which I thank you heartily, show that you are resigned. I have to ask her forgiveness for many things, but I do not doubt she will grant it, nor that she will greet me in another life, when these sufferings are ended, as she did at the station when I returned from the campaign in 1866 ; and I often long for this time.

But my great wish is first to see the great work finished in which I am called to help. And before this can be, we shall have to fight great battles, and difficulties which have to be overcome, surround us on all sides. But the Lord who has helped us so far, will continue His help.

I must send you my best wishes for Christmas, although for us it will always be connected with a

time of sadness.   The Lord took Marie to Himself
on the day when salvation was brought to mankind.

I thank Fritz for the welcome present of a foot-
bag, which is a bivouac in itself.   I have nothing
better to send from here than a case of champagne,
this I do, however, requesting you to empty it.

HELMUTH.

Mülhausen, August 17th, 1872.

At Munich we saw the opera, " The Huguenots,"
which was very well given, but we went home
before the last act, as I had to leave the following
morning at six o'clock.   At Kempten we found the
whole town assembled at the station, as the Crown
Prince had just arrived from Hohenschwangan.
He introduced me to a short gentleman in undress,
who was no one else than—the King of Naples,
an exiled monarch, whose deposition was caused
indirectly by the victories of the German Army
over Austria and France.   He had now to witness
an ovation to a German general, which he did with
great dignity.   I too received some of the " hurrahs."
At Linden, immense enthusiasm, girls clad in white,

flowers, &c. Here the Crown Prince was received by the Grand Duke of Baden, who insisted upon my coming to the Mainau. The crossing to the charming island on the lake of Constance in beautiful weather was delightful, and our stay there was made most agreeable by the happy family life of the excellent Grand Duchess and her children. Her Majesty the Empress was there, and very gracious. The following morning, after a family breakfast, the Grand Duke sent me by carriage to Constance, whence I travelled by rail through the lovely country close to the Falls of the Rhine at Schaffhausen by Basle to Mülhausen.

Innspruck, October 16th, 1875.

With Paul Groterjahn I say very contentedly, "Now we are here," i.e. at a tolerably good hotel in a room with a fire. It rained continually all the way from Berlin, and was so cold that I could not sleep during the night. This train, the express to Munich, is altered during the winter months; it begins about midnight to slacken speed, and instead of reaching our destination at

6 a.m., we did not arrive till 11 a.m. I at once went to see Professor Lenbach who has three unfinished portraits of me; the best, when finished, he will send to the Berlin exhibition. In the evening I went to the theatre with de Claer. We saw the "Fledermaus," a scandalous French comic opera, clumsily played by German actors.

We continued our journey at nine o'clock to-day; the rain resumed its business. At the station we met Steinäcker, Winterfeldt, and Lindequist of the Emperor's suite, and we travelled in the same carriage. The Secretary of State, v. Bülow, and Count Bismarck were also in the train. Prince Bismarck is not coming. We could see but little of the charming country, only now and then the clouds parted and allowed us a glimpse of the mountains freshly powdered over with snow. Kufstein, the Austrian fortress on the Bavarian side, is beautifully situated. Two mountain-forts with mighty towers and numerous loopholes command the narrow valley of the Inn. At present they are principally used for State prisoners, who can enjoy this beautiful country.

As the weather is so bad we shall not do much

more than visit the cathedral. In the middle of the nave stands the monument of the Emperor Maximilian I., the last of the knights ; on either side are eight-and-twenty gigantic bronze statues, most of them ancestors of the Emperor. The statue of King Arthur must be by Peter Vischer. This is a figure with such life and reality that one might imagine him walking about during the night amidst his iron neighbours.

Milan, October 20th.

On the 17th, the Emperor arrived at Innspruck, where he was received with every mark of honour, but the immense crowd observed a deep silence, and this was the case throughout the whole of the German Tyrol. The weather became clearer the farther south we went. The journey over the Brenner is very picturesque. In an ascent of 40 : 1 the railway makes such numerous and sharp curves that one sees the country all round as well as if one were driving. There is generally a great abyss on one side. At the top of the pass I remembered the inn with a broad roof, one gutter of which drains into the Black Sea, the other into the Adriatic. From this point the descent is so winding that some of the gentlemen reached the next station quicker on foot than we by train. Now the vegetation begins to show a southern character, first walnut-trees and vines, at Botzen fig-trees and cypresses. At Trent we dined at 7 p.m.; by moonlight we saw the well-laid-out streets, and the fortress-like Bishop's palace, where 300 years ago the Council of Trent was held, whose settlements the infallible pope will no longer recognize. The inn where I stayed must have been an old palace. The lofty hall, where the badly smelling stove gave no warmth, may have been occupied in former times by a high ecclesiastical dignitary.

We continued our journey on the 18th in bright sunshine. Passing the remarkable hermitage of Verona, we entered the plain of Lombardy. The whole garrison of Verona had marched out and paraded, and the forts saluted. If the people in the North Tyrol received us in silence, those in the South, on the contrary, were loud in their acclamations, which became even heartier when we entered Italy. We had a beautiful view of Lake Garda surrounded by snow-covered mountains, then the scenery became somewhat monotonous, fertile fields covered with mulberry-trees and vineyards and watered by canals, where the vine is trained in festoons.

From early morning we were *en grande tenue* with orders and ribands. At Bergamo we made our *déjeûner*, and at Milan the King met our Emperor at the station. In a long procession of more than twenty carriages we drove slowly through the beautiful streets, accompanied by the endless shouting of the dense crowd. The first presentations were followed by the banquet and the illumination of the cathedral with white, green and red lights. On the *Palazzo Reale*, adjoining the cathedral square, stood about 200,000 people closely packed; perfect order and quiet prevailed. No force of police could succeed like that in our country. Notwithstanding the population of Milan is very independent; nobody could force them to be enthusiastic; but the hurrahs were endless when the Emperor and the King stepped out on to the balcony. The well-known cathedral, built entirely of white marble, ornamented with more than a thousand statuettes, with innumerable spires and notches, is very impressive, and when lit up, quite fairy-like. Late at night de Claer and I, and General Taverna, who is in attendance on me, went (but incognito and in undress) through the magnificent gallery, which was illuminated by thousands of gas flames. Bands were playing on the squares, and the immense crowd went about quietly in perfect order without needing any control by the state "carabinieri." Such conduct is the fruit of ancient culture, perhaps only possessed by the Northern Italian. The unavoidable parade took place on the 19th. The battalions, formed in two ranks, numbered not more than three hundred and fifty men, who looked in good order and well disciplined. They defiled with eyes left, to enable the princesses and ladies to have a full view from a *loggia*. It was an impressive picture on the immense square near the old citadel.

I had caught a severe cold on the journey to Munich, became feverish and went to bed. Steinacker sent me some homœopathic drops. I only got up to attend the gala-dinner in the evening at seven o'clock. I had not been able to touch anything the day before, and after ten minutes in the Scala I had to drive home and lie down. The immense house, magnificently lit up, was an imposing sight. The boxes were let for as much as 800 francs, and in the first six rows everybody wore evening dress and white ties. Of course the Emperor was welcomed most enthusiastically. I have pretty well cured myself with sleep and starvation. But unfortunately a sirocco is blowing, and it rains continually. We drove to Monza, but the hunt did not come off. Even the beautiful park could only be seen from the castle. But I went on to the quaint old cathedral, where many treasures were shown to us; amongst others the iron crown with which forty-five Emperors have been crowned; the Emperor Francis being the last. Hidden by gold and jewels is an iron circle, made of the nails which fastened Jesus to the Cross.

October 21st. After coffee at 8 a.m., one does not feel very much inclined at 10 a.m. for a *déjeûner*, which is really a dinner. But after this had been endured and their Majesties had left for Monza, we had time to see Milan, beginning with the cathedral. Inside, through the soft subdued light, far away in the background, is seen a mighty golden cross. The full size of the cathedral does not appear at first. Its enormous length can only be realized from the steps of the high altar, underneath which lie the remains of the canonized Charles Borromeo. The vaulted ceiling, two hundred feet high, is beautifully painted, and has the effect of lace-work. When you have ascended an endless staircase and are out on the marble roof, a whole forest of tall spires and richly carved arches can be seen. On each little spire are a dozen saints; there are said to be seven thousand figures, but I have not counted them; each one is a work of art. A few more hundred steps bring you to the slender spire, and from here at a height of four hundred feet, all Milan can be overlooked; unfortunately, in spite of sunshine, the fog hid the Alpine chain, which is generally visible. After we had descended, luckily without any accident, we drove to St. Ambrogio, the oldest church of the city, unchanged and preserved in the pure Romanesque style of the fourth century. Count Taverna

showed us a well-preserved fresco portrait of his
ancestor with the inscription of his name. The
serpent of the Garden of Eden, the cause of all
our misery, can be seen here (in iron). Mass
books from the third century were shown to us;
also the crypt which was the refuge of the early
Christians, and numerous objects of beautiful
workmanship set with jewels. The gilt mosaics of
the apse remind one of those of St. Mark's at
Venice.

In one of the liveliest streets between the shops
and eating-houses a long row of pillars, the remains
of a temple of Minerva, have a very strange effect.
At the Brera we only saw the principal master-
pieces, above all the Sposalizio, by Raphael.
Among modern works, the portraits of Manzoni
and Cavour were interesting. In the afternoon I
had pleasant visits from General Cialdini, and
the Prime Minister, Minghetti.

In the room which I occupy the Consul Napoleon Buonaparte once stayed; the gilt bed is still
ornamented with the French eagles; the little room
adjoining, where Henry sleeps, was probably that
of his mameluke.

October 22nd. Last night there was a state ball; the enormous hall was lit up by several thousands of candles, and was densely crowded, when the Court and suite entered. Chairs, behind which the gentlemen stood, were placed for all the ladies in a large circle, so as to leave the centre free for the dancers. A linen drugget was spread on the floor, as it is not the fashion to have parqueted floors here. This circumstance and the trains of the ladies' dresses must render dancing very difficult; the Prussian gentlemen were the best dancers. It was impossible to move about, and at midnight I was glad to withdraw.

This morning King Victor Emmanuel sent his minister, commissioned to present me with a marble bust of His Majesty, larger than life-size. The king received me immediately afterwards, in undress and without ceremony. After a long and very friendly conversation, he said: " Embrassez-moi" and kissed me with his long moustache on both cheeks.

Our journey home is fixed for to-morrow; at Botzen we shall stay a night, but then we hope to arrive at Berlin in the afternoon of Monday, the 25th, without any further delay,

Your brother,

HELMUTH.

Rome, April 6th, 1876.

DEAR GUSTE,

While Henry is ascending the dome of St. Peter's, I can tell you something of our stay here instead of his doing so. We could not possibly have been received more amiably and courteously. We occupy a suite of rooms in Palace Caffarelli, provided with every possible luxury and comfort. On the writing-table before me stands Marie's photograph amidst roses and azaleas. On the left through the open door leading on to the balcony, through which the sun shines in brightly, the eye rests upon a garden of laurels, pine-trees, palms, and flowers; and farther away to the Palatine are seen the mighty ruins of Augustus' palace as large as the entire original Rome, behind which rise the Albanian mountains, with their wooded slopes, and the palaces and villas of Frascati and Grotta Ferrata.

Palace Caffarelli stands, as you may know, on the Capitoline hill, crowned in olden days by the Arx or Citadel, the taking of which was averted by the cackling of the geese. From the windows on the north side modern Rome is to be seen with its numerous churches and cupolas, palaces and spires as far as the mighty buildings of the Vatican, St. Angelo and St. Peter's. But from the south side are seen the Forum Romanum, the Colosseum, the triumphal Arches of Constantine, Trajan and Titus, the baths of Nero and Caracalla, the campagna with the arches of the aqueducts continuing for miles, in short, the whole past of the Eternal City.

Her future strength seems to be sought at the Quirinal; for while the Papacy tamely ends its tenacious life in voluntary exile, the capital of a richly gifted united people will become a new city with modern streets, gigantic ministerial buildings and barracks. These modern cloisters, with the rules and habits of their orders, their temporary celibacy and vows, are no hermitages. And the ancient Aurelian wall, 1500 years old, encloses even to-day all these contrasts, commencing with the

power of the Imperators, the constancy of the
Martyrs, the victory and the secularization of
the Papacy, and finally the moral idea of the
State. In other cities present times have wiped
away the past, here we find them both together.

King Victor Emmanuel is staying at present
at a country-house not far from Florence, but the
Crown Prince has granted me an audience for
to-day in the Quirinal. On the afternoon of our
arrival we met the Princess, as we drove to the
Milvian Bridge. She was walking, and knew us at
once, and it was impossible to remain incognito any
longer; the Minister of War has ordered Count
Taverna to be my attaché, as he was at Milan. We
hope that Herr von Keudell will return here from
Berlin next Sunday. Meanwhile, his wife provides us with everything necessary and agreeable;
she is very attentive and kind to us.

Hoping that you may derive much benefit from
Marienbad,

I remain,

Your brother,

HELMUTH.

Rome, April 19th, 1876.

Dear Guste,

Your letter of the 12th brought me very welcome news from home, and I send you my best thanks. I think of leaving for Naples (where I hope it will be warmer) on Friday or at the latest Saturday. We should not like to take too much advantage of the kindness of the dear Keudells. Nobody could be treated better than we have been this last fortnight. We have promised to be present to-morrow at a festival of the German artists here. And after that will be the best time to end our stay.

Bulwer's "Last Days of Pompeii" will interest me much, when we have seen, which I hope will be soon, the new excavations and the offender Vesuvius. The great museum, Mother Earth, has carefully preserved in her bosom a whole town as it disappeared, in one day, eighteen hundred years ago, in the midst of life. The past has here been discovered *in flagranti*, and has been brought to light again.

Of my Milanese friends, I have met Menabrea, Cialdini and Bertole Viale again. I have also made the acquaintance of the new ministers Depretis and Mezzacapo, who were all invited to *déjeûner* at the Keudells'.

The sun shines warm and bright through the windows, the freshest green covers the wide campagna as far as the eye reaches. There are the ruins of a past world, high arches of endless aqueducts and numerous monuments, which served as fortresses in the middle ages, and as swallows build, so the paltry life of the present has reared its huts under the protection of these mighty remains.

Under our balcony is a whole forest of azaleas in blossom; round the fountain "Die Myrthe still und hoch der Lorbeer steht," a palm planted by Frederick William IV., looks rather melancholy in the wind, and a white and red climbing rose covers everything with thousands of blossoms. It calls me into the open air, and so I conclude with a hearty greeting.

HELMUTH.

Naples, May 2nd, 1876.

DEAR GUSTE,

I will try if I can write a few lines to you with one of these dreadful steel-pens,[1] before our departure, fixed for to-morrow. Henry has climbed up to the convent of S. Martino, which I could not undertake to do on account of my asthma. My greatest pleasure has been to cross the bay by steamer. When we went to Capri the sea was rather rough, and some ladies made their sacrifice to Neptune; and under the steep rocky coast the deep-blue sea threw up its snow-white surge. The ship anchored and a number of little boats rocked about us to take us to the blue Grotto. This seemed impossible to me, for I saw distinctly the big waves beating against the upper part of the entrance, which was only three or four feet above the level of the sea in calm water. However, it was to be attempted. We lay down flat at the bottom of the nut-shell, and the practised rowers seized the moment between one wave and another. " Coraggio per voi, Maccaroni per noi ! " they cried out and—clash — we had passed the

---

[1] Moltke always used quills.

opening of the cavern, but not without my hat being turned into a " chapeau claque."

The very narrow entrance prevents the light entering the high spacious vault, which is about a hundred paces deep; this rocky cavern is lit up by the reflection of the sun-beams from the crystal light blue sea, and the effect is enchanting. But the idea of having to return again, prevented me from enjoying the sight in comfort. The foaming billows dashed in, barring the way; sometimes travellers have waited here two days for a calm sea. But by the dexterity of the boatmen, in waiting for the right moment, we soon found ourselves outside again, but were so wet that we could shake the water from our clothes. Very few of the passengers undertook this visit.

It is very trying for me, after going down to the beautiful walk near Villa Reale, on the seashore, to go up again one hundred and sixty steps to my house. But the wonderful view over the shore is an ample reward for the trouble. Each window has a marble balcony. On our left we see on a height, the sombre castle of St. Elmo, with its gloomy walls and battlements, just oppo-

site us we have Vesuvius, which towers high above
the many flat roofs and cupolas of the city; just
now only a white cloud of smoke is to be seen,
nothing remarkable. To the right the eye sweeps
over the bay as far as Castellamare and Sorrento,
where, in spite of the distance of three German
miles, single houses can be distinguished in a
clear atmosphere. Vesuvius is as quiet as if it had
never devastated whole towns and districts; we,
therefore, did not favour it with a visit, but only
looked from the foot at the black ashy cone.
One of the most beautiful things, I can imagine,
is the road that leads from Castellamare along high
rocky walls to the charming Sorrento. Deep
ravines cut perpendicularly into the white tuffa,
and are crossed by viaducts; far beneath lies
the blue sea fringed by the silvery surf which
dashes against most marvellous blocks of rock.
The mountains, almost to their summits, are
covered with olive trees; convents, and country
houses peep out; while the houses on the roadside
are hidden by orange bushes, which just now are
in full bloom, but still bear a great number of
their golden fruit. Stepping out of their shade

you suddenly find yourself on a platform of one of the many good inns ; before you is a precipice a hundred feet straight down to the glistening sea, to which underground paths lead down.

I think that we shall stay at Lucerne on our way home and take a few days' rest there. We should be glad to receive news from you there ; tell us also what kind of weather you have, and about the crops. It would be a pity to miss the time of blossom at Creisau. Friendly greetings also for my faithful de Claer.

Your brother,

HELMUTH.

Stettin, Sept. 23rd, 1879.

DEAR GUSTE,

We have just returned from the great review of the Second Army-Corps. Everything went off excellently. The weather yesterday, cold and wet, has turned into most beautiful sunshine, no dust and a pleasant, fresh air. I was in trouble about my great brown horse, which was so badly trained, that I could not use him in such a crowd. I therefore borrowed Henry's chestnut, which performed his part excellently. The thing is, amidst the noise of drums and bands and the waving of flags, to ride past His Majesty at a slow pace, then immediately to ride at full gallop to his side, which is not so easy as it looks, if the horse has not been trained for it.[1] The bearing of the troops was excellent; the Emperor was much pleased. As at Königsberg and Dantzic we have good quarters here, beautiful large rooms in an old patrician house on the Rossmarkt, excellent beds, with more to eat and drink than is good for us. The daily dinner with the King is every time a trial of self-denial for me; one dinner now and then I might be able to digest, but when it comes to twenty-one, one after another, I have to be very careful, especially with the many different kinds of wine. The festivities which follow one after another are much more exhausting than the manœuvres. On Sunday a man-of-war will be launched, and then there will be a gala-dinner. With much love,

Your brother,

Helmuth.

[1] Moltke had to parade his regiment, the Colberg Grenadiers, before His Majesty.

Schlettstadt, Oct. 3rd, 1879.

DEAR GUSTE,

I received the last news from you at Stettin. Since then the manœuvres at Strassburg and the Emperor's journey have come to an end. At first I was very doubtful if I could go through with everything. But, God be thanked, all went well, though only with the utmost exertion, and I hope it will have been for the last time. Now I can spare myself a little more, but I wish and long to pass the short time that is left to me in quiet, and to be allowed to retire into modest solitude. The future, and not, perhaps, a very distant one, may bring circumstances with which I feel no longer able to grapple.

I think Henry will have told you of our excursions to the Vosges Mountains. We had a cloudy day, but it cleared up towards evening, and we could see from the highest wooded point the valleys with their villages and many old castles on the mountain tops. The high-roads are so skilfully constructed with many windings along the mountain slopes, that one can drive down at a sharp trot without using the drag. If the sun

would only shine we should make some more excursions of the kind which can be combined with
our duties. Best love.

Your brother,

Helmuth.

Gastein, August 15th, 1880.

Dear Guste,

The sad news in the papers of floods and
destructions may have made you anxious about
us. We arrived here at noon, though not without
some trouble, yet well and sound. It is a good
thing that we did not go to the Tatra mountains,
for just in that direction the destruction has been
greatest.

The first day of our journey passed without
much disturbance. As Hôtel Wunsch had been
specially recommended to us, we stayed there, and
it was a strange coincidence that not only did I
occupy the same hotel, but also the same room
where I had been ill with fever for six weeks forty
years ago, on my return from Turkey. The following day we spent in going about Vienna, and we got

through a great deal. On Thursday we drove, in
torrents of rain, through a delightful country to
the beautiful Lake Traun. Hoping to be able to
cross this charming lake on the following day, we
passed the night at Gmunden, in the excellent new
Hôtel Austria, but the next morning it was still
raining and the Traunstein was wrapt in clouds.
However, in spite of that, the passage was beautiful.
But when we had landed at Ebensee, we were
received with the disagreeable news that the Traun
had interrupted all further communication ; that
the railway was destroyed, and the high-roads
flooded several feet deep. But we succeeded in
obtaining a carriage for a good deal of money,
and drove to our destination. The Mayor of the
place took a seat on the box and—God knows
what made him do so—waded in the worst places
before us up to his waist. A poor lad was taken
with us, who had to walk, where the road seemed
dangerous, before the horses. So we arrived at.
Ischl, but no train could leave there, and we stayed
the night. The whole platform was under water,
and the stream presented an interesting sight.
Débris of bridges swam past with tremendous

rapidity. In the evening there was a concert in
the casino, where we heard the comforting news
that an express would try to leave on the following
Wednesday. Fortunately it was true. Next
morning we were very glad to see the sun again ;
we took a lovely walk, and left at noon. The
saloon carriage which we occupied was open and
the last one on the train, so that we could look
over the whole country. It was the most
beautiful journey that one can imagine ; passing
by the Halstätter lake, then ascending between
lofty mountains by the foaming Traun, after
that, rapidly descending into the valley of the
Enns. Again floods and rain ; and then a descent
of more than a thousand feet into the valley of the
Salzach. Night quarters at Lend, which were as
bad as they were dear. This morning we passed
the Klamm on foot, and then waited for the *diligence*, which brought us here safe and sound at
half-past one o'clock. For old acquaintance's sake
I took a little room at Hôtel Straubinger. The
day after to-morrow I go into good apartments on
the ground floor. We have already looked about
a good deal, taken tea, and played at patience to

see if the weather was going to turn fine ; they all came right ; nevertheless it is raining still.

With best love to all, your brother,

HELMUTH.

Creisau, July 30th, 1881.

DEAR GUSTE,

I did not find any letter from you awaiting me yesterday on my return home. However, I hope that you are getting on well at Heligoland. The Tatra mountains are very interesting, but there is no comfort, either in food or lodging. We had to be content with one little room, and we were fortunate to get even that. Young Prince Leopold, who arrived with Colonel Geissler and his physician, was also quartered in a garret. Of course, I did not climb the high mountains, but was content with some excursions in the valleys. The journey by train through a beautiful country was lovely. Here everything is in good order.

HELMUTH.

SELECTIONS FROM LETTERS TO HIS SISTER MAGDALENE.

MAGDALENE VON MOLTKE, by her family always called Lene, the sixth child and the eldest daughter of her parents, was born on September 29th, 1807, at Augustenhof in Holstein. She lived devoted to her beloved mother until the death of the latter. When her mother's household was thus broken up, she went to live with her father, then Governor at Kiel, and remained his faithful companion till, in 1838, she was married to a clergyman, Mr. Bröker, the principal preacher at the Klosterkirche at Uetersen. This happy marriage was ended on June 12th, 1890, by the death of her husband. Lene's acquaintances were not many, but those who knew her, loved

and esteemed her on account of her mental gifts, her brightness, her self-denial, noble truthfulness, and deep Christian
humility. Her brother Helmuth was her pride; she, however,
never boasted of him. His indefatigable love and care made
her life and those of her family happy even after his death.
Frau Bröker died on January 3rd, 1892.

Berlin, December 9th, 1866.

DEAR BRÖKER,

   . . . You are right in saying that God's
grace has been visibly with us during the great
decisive events of last year. More than ever I have
learned to understand how God " is strong in the
weak." May the many things which still remain
to be done, succeed under His gracious guidance.

My wife sends her very best love to you and
her Aunt Lene. I hope we shall soon come to
Holstein again, and then it will be to the annexed
country. Till then we wish to be kindly remembered. Most affectionately yours,

HELMUTH V. MOLTKE.

Wildbad, October, 12th, 1868.

DEAR LENE,

   . . . I hope that the treatment here which
will come to an end in a few days, will strengthen

me for all that next spring may bring. Our old King may have a hard trial before him; however, it is to be hoped that sound common sense will conquer the pride of our neighbours.

We must leave it to God Almighty.

I am very glad that the King has been so much liked in the Duchies. The secret of his pleasantness is his honest, open character. . . . My visit here is very late this year. . . . The country is very pretty, but, like the whole of the Black Forest, there is too much sameness. Beautiful green valleys watered by the rushing Enz, closed in by mountains which are covered with forests of high, thick, dark firs. The baths are delicious. Numerous warm springs bubble out from the floor of the basin at a temperature of twenty-seven degrees R. The cooking here is excellent; one could not dine better in Paris; trout from the stream, turbots from Marseilles, artichokes from Algiers. Railway communication makes everything easy.

We mean to leave to-morrow, first for the Palatinate. . . .

Marie joins me in best love to you.

HELMUTH.

Berlin, December 18th, 1875.

DEAR LENE,

. . . May your health improve again, and may you have a happy old age free from care. When one reaches an age such as we, who are left, have attained, one can bear many little physical sufferings patiently, if God only gives us peace in ourselves.

All of us wish you and Bröker and all your family a happy Christmas. After to-morrow the days will begin to lengthen again, and God will give us a new spring which I look upon every time as a special blessing. I hope we may see you next year at Creisau, where I enjoy life more than anywhere else. Though farming is not very profitable, I rejoice in the growth of the trees that I have planted, and under the shade of which the young generation will think of me when I have found a home of peace in the chapel there, which time cannot be very far off.

With heartiest love, your brother,

HELMUTH.

Berlin, September 18th, 1876.

DEAR LENE,

Uncle Ludwig and the four giants[1] will go on the 2nd of next month to Parchim to be present at the unveiling of my monument. Ludwig will have to give an address, and the four giants, I suppose, will be posted at the four corners of the pedestal. I shall, on the same day, be at Strassburg at the unveiling of a monument in memory of the fallen warriors, at which the Emperor has promised to be present. After that I hope to return to Creisau and to spend the month of October there. God bless you. Your faithful brother,

HELMUTH.

Creisau, June 30th, 1878.

DEAR LENE,

. . . I am sorry to say that I shall have to leave the country in August or September, as I shall have to attend the Reichstag, where we are going to attack the democrats.

---

[1] Thus the Field-Marshal liked to call the sons of his brother Adolf.

The recovery of the Emperor is steady, but slow, and it is still very doubtful if he will be able to be present at the coming manœuvres on the Rhine. It is not a little thing to receive thirty-one shots at the age of eighty-one. The responsibilities of a ruler already weigh upon the Crown Prince. The attempt upon the Emperor and the loss of the Great Elector [1] were two serious misfortunes! . . .

To-day the first stubbles! the rape-field is cut, and now the corn-harvest will begin. It promises to be very good, but even the best yields but a poor return. However, the estate improves every year. I intend to build some new workmen's houses this year.

You would be delighted to see the infants' school; the day-school too is prospering. Eighty-five little capitalists have savings-bank books, and everyone has some marks in the Provincial Savings Bank. It is so important to learn to save at an early age, as we know from our own experience. Our new generation has begun life with help,

---

[1] A man-of-war.

which none of us Sisters and Brothers have ever known.

And now farewell, dear Lene. Your

HELMUTH.

Berlin, December 24th, 1878.

DEAR LENE,

May you spend this Christmas in health and contentment. For me these are days of sad remembrance. Just ten years ago Marie fell ill, and was taken away in the prime of life. It is wonderful with what love she is remembered by comparative strangers, such as small artisans or merchants; her simple, genial manner is never forgotten. Only quite lately somebody spoke to me about her asking me for her photograph. And you too were so fond of her.

I am well; I have much to do, and that helps one to forget many a sorrow, and no one is without one.

You will have seen enough in the papers about the safe return of our Emperor, and the grand festivities on his arrival. Your brother,

HELMUTH.

Schlettstadt, October 3rd, 1879.

DEAR LENE,

I have just received your letter, and am glad that at your age you are so well and strong. Many happy returns of the day ; may you always spend it surrounded by children and grand-children.

As Schlettstadt may not find a place in your geography, I will tell you that I am south of Strassburg in Alsace, where I have been travelling with thirty officers and fifty horses, since the Imperial visit to this part of the Empire. The country between the Rhine and the Vosges is very fine, beautiful forest-land between lovely emerald meadows, and mountains crowned with ruins of old castles. The towns, and even the villages, are surrounded by walls and provided with splendid churches. Strangely enough, as long as the Emperor travelled here the weather was uninterruptedly fine, and the very day his journey ended, it began to rain, and has since rained every day.

My journey may last ten or fourteen days longer ; undoubtedly it will be the last of the kind.

I am now almost eighty years old, and I am no longer strong enough for such work. It is astonishing how the Emperor can still do what he does.

Henry accompanies me on my journey, keeps my accounts and also me in order. Your brother,

HELMUTH.

Berlin, March 18th, 1881.

DEAR LENE,

What do you think of the dreadful attempt on the Czar of Russia, who has been the greatest benefactor to his country ! It is to be hoped that his successor may take stricter measures against this vile band of Nihilists, and not hush up and pardon every crime as his unfortunate father has done. But he has a heavy task to take up. The people demand free institutions and representation for which they are not ready ; even their deputies can neither read nor write. Our Emperor is deeply shaken and affected by the loss of his nephew, who was attached to him with affectionate love and veneration. With best love, your brother,

HELMUTH.

Berlin, March 30th, 1883.

DEAR LENE,

Ernestine has informed you of the sad news of the passing away of our dear Sister Guste. This evening a service will be held over her remains at Potsdam, and to-morrow night the coffin will be taken to Creisau, where it will be deposited in the little chapel. There will then be left room enough for myself between both of them. She was seventy-four, and only had to struggle with death during a few hours' illness; that is a great grace of God. . . .

Most heartily,

HELMUTH.

Creisau, September 8th, 1886.

DEAR LENE,

I have passed a beautiful time here, the whole of the summer; it only passes too quickly.

. . . . Wilhelm's Helmuth is a fine boy, plain, with long ears like mine, but sturdy and strong and not easily kept in order by anybody but his father. The other day he did not come in time for dinner in spite of the bell, and only after searching for a long time was he found near the mill-pond, where he was catching fish with his Sunday hat. The second, Joachim Peter, is a picture of a boy.

Helmuth's eldest boy, Willy, is still a delicate child, but lively and clever. When the Peile had flooded the fields, he asked where all the water was running to, and when he was told that it went into the sea, he said: "But, papa, does the water know where the sea is?" With best love. Your brother,

Helmuth.

Berlin, December 19th, 1887.

Dear Lene,

The comfortable-looking Frau Pröbstin, in the excellent photograph, cannot be in bad health. The picture gives me much pleasure; I see a very striking likeness to our poor Father, just as I did in our brother Fritz, when he was old. You will find one of the two enclosed portraits, in a more meagre condition.

I wish you a joyful Christmas with all my heart.

Helmuth.

Berlin, March 2nd, 1888.

DEAR LENE,

The newspapers say all that I could tell you, about the sad time that we have lived through here in Berlin.

The death of the Emperor William has called forth the deepest sympathy of the whole world. It lay in the natural course of things, that the aged Monarch must be called away some day. He fell asleep without any struggle. His face had a mild, peaceable expression.

But truly tragical is the fate of his successor, who stands with one foot on the throne, the other in the grave. He bears his sufferings with a wonderful manliness; how long or how short this trial will be, God alone knows. In outward appearance he is still the same splendid, strong man.

The good old Empress Augusta keeps up well by her strength of will, in spite of feebleness and deep grief.

To-day we have mourning services in all our churches, instead of the birthday festivities, to which we had been accustomed for so many years. And everything is enveloped in a deep snow. The trees bend their branches under the weight of it, but the streets are beginning to thaw and are in a dreadful state in spite of the hundreds of snow-carts. . . .

With hearty greeting. Your brother,

HELMUTH.

Creisau, September 3rd, 1889.

DEAR LENE,

I suppose both of us are thinking with silent, but affectionate sympathy of our poor brother Ludwig. All I have heard of his last days seems comforting. He has passed away peacefully amid friendly surroundings.

Rosy will feel her father's loss most deeply; she has nursed him to the end, with most self-sacrificing love. She has promised to come to see us at Creisau, as soon as the most urgent arrangements have been made. Later on she will remain at Ratzeburg in the old home; Gustchen will also very likely keep her present position with Princess Albrecht.

I have just bought a second estate, Werners-dorf, near the Zobten, and have let it to Ludwig Moltke. I think this is the best way of providing for my heirs ; for the conversion of shares, which may be expected in a short time, threatens all capitalists with a loss of a tenth or a fifth of their interest. Land brings little, but it can neither be converted, taken away, nor stolen. Please give my best love to Bröker. Your brother,

HELMUTH.

Berlin, May 1st, 1890.

DEAR LENE,

The grace of God has allowed us to live through another Spring, a beautiful gift for which we owe special thanks. At present there are only the gooseberry bushes and other little shrubs whose little green leaves open to the light, but every day adds something new and beautiful, and soon the old lime-trees in your garden will unfold their splendour.

I should much like to go to the country now

when reviving nature is so beautiful, but the
Reichstag will meet soon, and in the present un-
pleasant state of things, the presence of every
conservative element is much to be desired.
Therefore I must stay here.

Much love, from your brother,

HELMUTH.

FRIEDRICH JOACHIM VON MOLTKE.

SELECTIONS FROM LETTERS TO HIS BROTHER FRITZ.

FRIEDRICH JOACHIM VON MOLTKE, the Field-Marshal's second brother, was born on the 22nd of May, 1799, on the estate of Horst near Ratzeburg. He received his early education with his elder brother Wilhelm, and his younger brother Helmuth, in the house of Pastor Knickebein at Hohenfelde in Holstein. From 1811 to 1817 he and his brother Helmuth were at the College for Military Cadets, at Copenhagen; which he left at the age of eighteen, after having successfully passed the last examination. Twenty years later, when a captain, he left the Army to join the Postal Service in Denmark. After losing his wife, Elisabeth Boelte, who had been his faithful companion for thirty years, he retired as Postmaster at Flensburg and Danish Chamberlain. With his widowed sister, Auguste Burt, he made his home at Lübeck in 1867. But during the last years of his life he was again brought into close relationship with his brother Helmuth. Fritz Moltke was a thoroughly earnest character, possessed of great self-denial, strict with himself and ready to devote himself to others. Throughout his life, in all circumstances, he gained universal esteem by his great industry, his integrity, his sense of duty and his prudence. Brought up with his brother Helmuth in the strict school of the College of Cadets at Copenhagen, he had followed his quiet and laborious path in the Danish service, while the younger brother, led by his star into the old Fatherland, had found in Germany the glory which will always be associated with his name. Each of the brothers honoured the opinions of the other. Their political interests, which may sometimes have differed, could never alienate them.

Fritz, therefore, joyfully sacrificed himself, and, giving up his own household, joined his brother in Berlin, when the latter was left alone after the death of his wife in 1868. Here he became the Field-Marshal's adviser in all family affairs. Together they collected the scattered accounts of their family, and together they rejoiced in the establishment of a new family seat. The Field-Marshal always treated his brother with the greatest consideration, and showed by his manner that he never forgot he was the younger. Politics were not discussed between them.

When on the 4th of August, 1874, a quiet death put an end to the sufferings which Fritz von Moltke had borne with great resignation, the Field-Marshal, deeply moved, buried the remains of his brother in the beautifully situated cemetery of Flensburg by the side of his deceased wife.

Glion, near Montreux,

November 3rd, 1866.

DEAR FRITZ,

I received your letter dated the 18th of last month all right, and ought to have answered it before this, but you know that one has never less time than when one has nothing to do but to enjoy one's self. We have had a wonderful autumn ; for thirty-seven days we have only once had rain. This enabled me to take sixteen baths during the beginning of my stay at Ragatz, and I have derived much benefit from them.

We then went by Zurich and Fribourg (crossing the marvellous suspension bridge, three hundred feet above a wide valley) to the Lake of Geneva. The country is lovely, descending by train about two thousand feet, through woods and vineyards. After spending a few days at Ouchy, near Lausanne, we came here to Glion about a fortnight ago. We are staying at a " pension " which bears the name of " the Waadtländische Rigi " rightly. It is 1600 feet above the lake, which is itself 1200 feet above the level of the sea. The view, to the Savoy mountains, over the blue waters of the lake, and the continuous row of villages and country houses on its shores, is most enchanting. The air is so reviving that we daily ascend heights which reach up to the snow-line, and every time we are surprised by new views. Yesterday we walked in brightest sunshine above the clouds. Beneath us seemed to lie a white snow-field, from which only the rugged Juras and the snow-capped summits of the High Alps appeared.

I think you have done rightly in giving up your troublesome post. I am glad that you are leaving Flensburg where you would miss your usual occupation. I, too, like Lübeck very much, and I hope we shall come to see you there next year. How much I should like to retire before then, but it is uncertain whether circumstances will allow me to send in my resignation. Then we could spend next autumn together at Glion. Adieu, dear Fritz. With best love to Guste.

Your

HELMUTH.

Freiburg in Silesia.

July 24th, 1867.

DEAR FRITZ,

I have received your letter of the 20th of this month, also one from Guste, dated 19th inst.

I have seen some beautiful estates here, but the prices are exorbitant. The land here is sold at a hundred thalers the half ton,[1] and up to two hundred in small portions; as the soil is very fertile and in a high state of cultivation, rent is very high. I have not come to a conclusion as yet. Baron Richthofen will come to-morrow, he is my adviser, as I can judge of nothing but the situation and the house. But I have learnt this much, that two hundred thousand thalers (£30,000) will not do much where land is concerned.

I am surprised to hear from Guste that Marie's liver is out of order. I have never known her to be anything but strong and contented. It is, however, possible that she has inherited an inclination in that direction from her father, who suffered from his liver. I shall speak to the doctor as soon as I come back, and I am quite ready to go with

[1] Local measurement.

her to Karlsbad, but I am afraid she will laugh at me when I propose it.

I am glad to hear that you like Lübeck; I, too, am very fond of the old town with its spires and old lime-tree avenues. Have you happened to make the acquaintance of Senator Dr. Curtius? He is very devoted to me. We have had a beautiful ride through the lovely mountains. People are indescribably grateful here for the protection which they received last year. All the towns have hoisted flags; Mayors and Councils came to meet us at the gates; a fat alderman had his horses put in and came for miles to kiss my hand; the toll-gatherer on the high-road sent his little girl with a simple little nosegay, etc. On the 1st of August we shall be back in Berlin.

I have a letter from Mary from Segeberg. She, too, was much pleased with Lübeck. Now farewell, this must be enough for to-day, dear Fritz. Best love to Guste. Your brother,

HELMUTH.

Creisau, near Schweidnitz,

Autumn, 1867.

DEAR FRITZ,

I was very sorry not to be able to come to Lübeck on the 3rd of this month, as I had intended, but just at that time I had to make large payments for the purchase of my estate, Government stamps and legal expenses ; then we came here on the 10th inst. to make the necessary arrangements in the new house, and to become generally acquainted with our new surroundings ; and all this prevented me from writing. In the country there are such a number of things to be done, the day is over in no time, and tired out we retire gladly to bed in the evening.

Up to the present I have only experienced the expense which the possession of an estate incurs, and I shall have to get accustomed to it. Seven hundred thalers (105*l.*) for artificial manure, six hundred thalers (90*l.*) for new seed, the pay of the work-people, repairs, &c. ; in a few days we shall have the threshing-machine here, which costs twenty-five thalers (3*l.* 15*s.*) per day, but it threshes three hundred bushels of wheat per day, and enables us to put the straw into stacks in the fields. The harvest is so abundant this year that the barns, which are very extensive, cannot hold it all.

Everybody congratulates me on my purchase at the cost of about three hundred thalers (45*l*.) per ton of land. The soil is most fertile, of great depth, and pays the best in the country, but was formerly very much neglected, and is not yet in the best condition; it therefore needs, for the present, the artificial help of chemical manure (superphosphate). The situation between the Zobten on the north, and the " *hohe Eule* " on the south side is charming. I have taken my carriage and a riding-horse with me, and it is delightful to drive out after the heat of the day is over. The whole country is like a garden, and wherever one drives it is beautiful. There are very good roads, and the hilly ground affords endless change of scenery and many views. We have very pleasant neighbours who have received us with the greatest kindness. The day before yesterday I took my seat, for the first time, in the assembly of the Kreistag. We should so much like to have you and Guste here, and we invite you most heartily and pressingly. We are putting off the longer excursions into the mountains till you come. You would be a great help to me, for I have all kinds of plans : an alteration of the Schloss, a bridge over the Peile, the laying-out of a park by making paths through fields and wood, the planting of trees, etc., etc. I have sent for a little surveying apparatus, and mean to begin with drawing a plan of the land which I intend for the park. But there are too many things to be done.

Since my arrival here we have had most beautiful harvest weather, and the whole day long heavy corn waggons, laden with wheat, cross the yard and draw up at the barns. Everything is built of stone. The vaulted roof of the sheep-shed is supported by twenty granite columns. But the "Schloss" has a shingle roof and must have one of slate, which will cost two thousand thalers (300*l.*). Last night we had a thunder-storm and the first rain, which was very favourable for the rape-seed. I do not think that they will be able to carry anything to-day ; but they can plough. There is never any want of work here. I have agreed to a larger allowance of meat to the farm labourers, to keep them strong and make them willing. They are a very fine race of people.

I think country-life here will interest you ; and as you are free at last and your own master, I hope you will not refuse my request to come. We send our best love.   Your brother,

HELMUTH.

Berlin, Dec. 29th, 1867.
DEAR FRITZ,

. . . The movement towards the incorporation of Lauenburg ought to come from the members of the Duchy. Our Parliament desires annexation, but the Government can take no steps until the Duchy expresses such a wish. I do not see how Ludwig under these circumstances can get an appointment in Lauenburg. This difficulty of finding suitable work is another drawback in small states.

The King has given me his large photograph for a Christmas present; I think you have seen it here at Schnäbely's.

Farewell, dear Fritz. Your brother,

HELMUTH.

Berlin, January 24th, 1868.

DEAR FRITZ,

. . . In Prussia, during these troublous times
it is much more difficult to help the ruined landowners and farmers than the starving work-people,
who are looked after extremely well.   Collections
are being made at home and abroad.   The order of
the Knights of St. John will provide considerable
sums, and even Marie is very busy with a bazaar
to be held in the castle.   But the work provided by
the State is of far greater importance ; 15 millions
are to be spent in the construction of a railway.
Of course, this cannot change the dreadful climate
of this province, which has such a rich soil.   All
field labour has to be done during the few summer
months, even building is stopped in the winter.
When we begin the ploughing in Silesia, the sow-
ing has to be finished in Prussia, as snow and frost
are beginning then.   This necessitates a compara-
tively large stock of utensils, and many workmen
and horses, who all have to be kept through the
long winter.

At midsummer, after a year's experience, I
shall be able to form some idea of the net profit

of the estate.   Of course, in future, we could not expect the same high price for the corn.   Marie's kitchen is always amply provided with butter, hares, geese, and pork from Creisau.   Much love from both of us to Guste.

Helmuth.

Berlin, January 27th, 1868.

Dear Fritz,

I am learning at Creisau what a small income land produces in our times, even under the most favourable circumstances.   Though the price at 120 thalers (18*l.*) the acre is thought very reasonable by all competent judges, I shall be quite satisfied if, at the end of the year, my capital brings in $2\frac{1}{2}$ per cent. interest ; but I hardly expect it will. He who wants a higher rate, must not invest his money in land.   But in spite of every drawback, there is nothing like landed property.   It will always be the safest investment, while shares are affected by the fluctuations of politics and the exchange which, of course, depend finally on the value of land and the security it gives.   The great landowners represent the highest rank in every country. Even the income of this estate will place my successor in a good position, and it will probably be increased through the improvements we hope to make, and when the debt has been paid off.

I think the whole income of Creisau will at present have to be spent on necessary improvements, as a new roof, the laying out of the park, improvement of the fields, etc.; of course, if this is done, it will be all the better for my successor. The remainder of my income will be sufficient for myself and the support of relations, but I shall not be able to increase my capital much.

Ludwig's resignation has been accepted. He will receive a pension, the title of "Privy Councillor" and, I think, a decoration of some kind. Adolf has been nominated Landrath in the district of Pinneberg-Rantzau, and I hope that after the dissolution of the Landtag, which will take place in a few days, the position and salaries of the officials in Holstein will be definitively settled. With much love to Guste, your brother,

HELMUTH.

Berlin, March 7th, 1868.

DEAR FRITZ,

I am quite satisfied with Creisau. I knew beforehand that I could not expect high interest, when I invested my capital in land; it would have been the same in Holstein. I should have liked to settle there, but I did not hear of anything suitable at the time that I wanted to buy. The principal thing for me is the safety of the investment, not high interest. If I wished to increase it, I could easily do so by realizing. You see a danger in the depreciation of land, but that only affects those who are obliged to sell. With entailed property this does not come into consideration. If stocks and land become depreciated it does not alter the rate of interest nor the income. Of course, it is an advantage for the buyer under such circumstances. As the income would remain the same, his capital would bring double the interest. This has already happened with Austrian, Russian and American bonds of 5 per cent, which can be bought for fifty, which means investing one's capital at 10 per cent. If I could have bought Creisau for half the sum I paid, the income

of the estate would have been the same, but I
should have received double the interest.   But the
difference is this, that if invested in shares, the
capital itself is endangered ; for if milliards double
or treble, the necessary consequence will be the
bankruptcy of the state, which has occurred several
times in Austria, and will occur in America.
Landed property can be devastated by war and
misfortunes, but the soil cannot be carried away,
and its productiveness remains unchanged, at
least, as far as earthly things can be unchangeable.
Though the Hamburg merchants know quite well
the value of stocks and shares, yet they like to
invest their savings in property in Holstein, which
only brings in two per cent.

I have never heard a word of gratitude in
Holstein from anybody for having been freed from
the Danish Government, which was always described as ignorant and tyrannical. The people
in Silesia are very grateful to those who averted
the danger which threatened them. We have
had quite touching proofs of it. My name is
much honoured there, and that too is of value.
The railway does away with distance, and those

who wish to come to us will not make a two days'
journey an excuse.

If Adolf should retire, it would be a good thing
to buy the Dreskys' pretty house on the hill and
to keep it always as a dower house.

Much love to Guste. Marie joins me in love to
yourself.

HELMUTH.

Berlin, May 14th, 1868.

DEAR FRITZ,

I have duly received the pedigree. The
accounts which I had, not a very long time ago,
from relations living in Würtemberg, agree with
it perfectly. It would be very interesting to know
where the estates, which are mentioned in different
places, as for instance, Westerbrügge, which remained in the family for several generations, are
situated. It is remarkable that Stridfeld (Meck-
lembourg) which remained in the branch of Claus
v. Moltke for eleven generations, is, in the four-
teenth generation, found in the possession of the
family of Otto (Samow) owned by Joachim (the
father of Count Adam) of Walkendorf and Ehren-

reich of Walkendorf. Both died in 1730, and yet the estate remained in this branch, though there were male heirs of the former living. At all events, it is seldom that an estate, not entailed, descends from 1309 to 1781, for almost five hundred years, and through fifteen generations, in the same family.

As far as I have been able to see from the names of the estates, real Danish branches have only existed since 1730. The sons of all the Moltkes that were known in Denmark before that time, have always returned to the Mecklenburg soil.

I had hoped that you and Guste would visit us at Creisau, and that you would inspect my new park. I expect to be there at the end of June or in July; but it will not be safe to make plans for the next few weeks. La France s'ennuye! and in order to amuse her, Europe must be set on fire. In the nineteenth century a war so frivolously begun, to so little purpose, should seem impossible, it reminds one of Louis XIV. and his Louvois, and yet we stand, perhaps, close upon it. All depends upon the decision of an irresolute man, who continually excites the national passions on purpose and in such a way that the country cannot tolerate the budget much longer ; a man who cannot decrease the Army without losing the good opinion of the public, especially of the Army itself, and who will have to lead this Army to be slaughtered, in order to rid himself of it. The situation seems to me very serious. With hearty love, your brother,

Helmuth.

Berlin, December 6th, 1868.

Dear Fritz,

I am glad that you have found an easy way of investing your money. It would be strange if the Exchange of a commercial town like Lübeck were not provided with Prussian Government Consols. Very likely they are numerous there. You must not be astonished if the four-and-a-half per cent. shares go down to three and a half. In Prussian railway shares alone, forty millions have been thrown away in the money market. But much cash is sent to Russia. Russian railway shares nominally bring five per cent, but as they do not sell for more than seventy-five, they really bring seven per cent. Though these lines are useful for military purposes and administration in general, it seems doubtful to me if they will ever pay, as they are laid down through real deserts. But the advantage of a safe income for a time makes people overlook the danger, which they have already experienced with Spanish and Austrian shares. However, such events show the value of greater security, and the Prussian Government shares will probably rise in a very short time.

I think Lübeck will have a good Mayor in Curtius; I am very glad that he has received this token of confidence from his fellow-citizens.

Since I have seen the ghostly form of the celebrated violinist Ernst at Gastein, I am convinced that music and nothing but music, and especially violin playing, is ruinous to the nerves. It would probably be a good thing for Ludwig and his daughters to exchange the musical and poetical land of dreams for real life. A few months' stay in the beautiful neighbourhood at Creisau would do all of them good. It has been offered to them repeatedly. Marie joins me in love to yourself and Guste.   HELMUTH.

Berlin, January 8th, 1869.[1]

DEAR FRITZ,

You will have learnt from my letter to Guste how pleased I am with the plan of our living together, and how I value the sacrifice which you are thus making for me. But I feel that I must remind you again of one fact connected with it, namely, that I occupy these rooms in an official capacity, and when I die they must be given up, in which case you would, of course, be obliged to move again.

If, in spite of this objection, you still like to keep to our arrangement, it will be best for you to settle at Creisau for good, for Creisau is the piece of earth which our family possesses; and pass the winter or, if you like, the greater part of the year in Berlin with me as a visitor. I hope to spend the spring and autumn at my country seat. In the autumn I have to attend the manœuvres and to travel on General Staff duty, which will take several weeks. During that time you could stay quietly in the country. I hope you

---

[1] After his wife's death which took place on December 24th, 1868.

will take everything there that has become dear
to you through old associations, as the house
is very roomy.   I shall be glad of everything you
like to have about you.

If you decide on joining me, I shall do everything in my power to assure you an independent
future.

HELMUTH.

Berlin in June, 1869.

DEAR FRITZ,

I received both your letters by the afternoon post, and I arranged everything at once.

Adolf said in his letter, that he was coming to
Creisau in the middle of July, but I am sorry to
say only for a fortnight. Nobody will thank him
for it, and nobody could blame him if he asked
for a six weeks' or three months' leave. I have
proposed to him to come and meet me as early as
the 20th inst., we could then travel by rail
together through the lovely mountains; but there
is nothing to be done with him; he thinks the sea-
surrounded country would fall to pieces if he did
not write certain documents himself.

I am getting on quite well and am glad that my loneliness will soon come to an end. I am very thankful to you for writing so frequently, it is almost as if I were with you. As it is late, I must conclude, and remain, with hearty greetings,

Yours,

HELMUTH.

Berlin, June 22nd, 1869.

DEAR FRITZ,

I had not gone to Bremen on official business, but had been ordered to Wilhelmshaven. However, I had accepted the invitation of the town, to be its guest, and the papers are full of intellectual things that I might have said, but which I did not say.

The King has dissolved the *Zollparlament* to-day in person.

With much love, and hoping much to see you again soon,

HELMUTH.

Reims, September 6th, 1870.

Wer zählt die Völker, wer nennt die Namen, die

K

gestern hier zusammen kamen![1] There stands the mighty Cathedral in which the Kings of France, Clovis, St. Louis, all the other Louis and Charles X., were crowned. Close by, in the Archbishop's palace, King William is staying now; in the large courtyard an armed company is bivouacing, and in the city a whole Army-corps is quartered. The cannon, munition-waggons and transport, are well arranged along the promenade. The large hotel opposite is crowded with officers, regaling themselves after their many bivouacs. We have been warned that the whole city is undermined with millions of bottles of champagne. It is not surprising that some hundreds of them exploded yesterday; nothing else could be expected in hot weather like this, and where there are so many thirsty throats. Everywhere friends met and greeted each other, but many a one was missed, who is resting now underneath the green turf. Of our friends from Creisau, I met Colonel v. Bock, Count Reichen-

---

[1] "Who counts the nations, knows the names." Well-known lines by Schiller. The last words are an addition made by Moltke.

bach, Lieutenant Goldammer; all were well. In
the evening our gardener came, and was glad to
see Augustus and Ernest. He has been attached
to the sanitary corps, and wears the red cross.
His corps, the sixth, has not been in any engagement as yet, nevertheless they will very likely be
the first to see the towers of Notre Dame. On
our way here, the day before yesterday, we passed
the camp of the Tenth Division, and found Helmuth with the officers of his regiment sitting
under an apple-tree. He looks a little thin, but
assured me he was perfectly well. He said he
had "plenty" of money; refused a sausage, and
was contented with a bottle of wine out of my
carriage. His coat tails were riddled with shot,
but he himself is unharmed, and in good spirits.
He will receive his promotion as an officer in a
few days.

Wilhelm is before Metz and will not allow
Bazaine to come out. One attempt had already
been made before his arrival. I think his only
course is to capitulate very soon. It will be quite
embarrassing to know what to do with 200,000
prisoners.

K 2

I think I have already told you, that I received
the painful commission of informing the French
plenipotentiaries, that MacMahon and his whole
Army had been taken prisoners, and that I had to
settle the conditions. These negotiations took place
from twelve to two o'clock, in the night after the
battle of Sedan. The following morning, General
Wimpffen, who was in command, after Mac-
Mahon was wounded, was to state definitely his
terms, but Napoleon came himself. I could not,
however, treat with him, as he was a prisoner of
war, having written to the King the day before :
" N'ayant pas pu mourir au milieu de mes troupes
il ne me reste qu'à remettre mon épée entre les
mains de Votre Majesté."   I met him in a
miserable peasant's hut, close behind our outposts,
in expectation of an interview with the King ; he
was in full uniform, sitting on a wooden chair.
When I entered, he rose and asked me to take a
seat, which was opposite him. To his proposals
I could only answer, that nothing less than the
capitulation of the whole Army was demanded,
and that I should have to give the signal for the
renewal of the firing, if the Army had not sur-

rendered before ten o'clock. " C'est bien dur," he sighed. But he was quiet and resigned to his fate. Soon after a capitulation, drawn up by us and translated, was signed without hesitation by the unfortunate Wimpffen. He had arrived from Africa only two days before, and he must have found his position at the head of the totally demoralized and terribly excited soldiers at Sedan a most trying one. But eighty cannon stood close before the town, with 150,000 men behind them. Wimpffen has received permission to go to Würtemberg, where he has relations (doubtless our cousin Käthchen belongs to the same family). He will never be forgiven in France for having signed the treaty, however innocent he may have been of the great catastrophe.

By-the-bye, he has thanked me by letter for the considerate manner in which these painful nego-tiations have been conducted.

On the following morning, a long row of carriages, escorted by a squadron of Black Hussars (the Death-Heads), drove in pouring rain through Donchery on the high-road to Bouillon (in Belgium). Count Bismarck looked out of the window on one side of the street, myself on the other ; the abdicated Emperor bowed, and a piece of the world's history was finished.

Everybody is anxious to know what will become of France ; no doubt a military republic. Meanwhile we shall march to Paris.

HELMUTH.

Reims, September 11th, 1870.

While our troops are making long marches on account of new operations, the Commanders-in-Chief have been allowed to remain in this ancient city, where the kings used to be crowned.

We all enjoy this rest, it will also be a boon to the horses, who have kept up wonderfully so far. The weather is bad, cold and damp ; we see nothing of the fine climate of France.

Wilhelm moves on to-morrow to besiege Toul, unless the cavalry is sent here to Reims. Helmuth is at present near Montmirail.

I hope you have had my two last letters from here, and that you will soon receive forty bottles of champagne which I have sent, and with which, I hope, you will drink the health of our brave troops.

By rights the war ought to be ended now as France has no longer an Army ; one has capitulated and the other will certainly have to do so. At Metz this is the twenty-fourth day that 200,000 mouths have had to be fed. We hear from the prisoners that they have begun to eat horse flesh. Bazaine may make another desperate attempt to cut through the lines, but all necessary precautions to prevent it have been taken. In Paris there are no other soldiers left but the incomplete corps Vinoy, and a very large number of *gardes nationales*, men who defend themselves behind ramparts and ditches, but who can never dare to come out and fight our men in the open field. The difficulty is that there is no authority with whom peace can be concluded. The present Government was established in this manner : at the last ridiculous meeting a workman jumped upon the president's chair, rang the bell and proclaimed the republic. What the rest of France and the wealthy classes think of it, we do not know.

Yesterday I drove with Henry and de Claer to

the forsaken camp near Châlons. A fortnight ago, when the 4th Cavalry division, the " *uhlans prussiens,*" who were known to have stormed villages on foot, were said to be advancing, the terror was so great that the whole Army Corps fled to Reims and in such haste, that our horsemen found half-served breakfasts, cannon, trunks, women's clothes, and letters just begun. Here all the walls are bored through to make loopholes, great entrenchments had been constructed, but they were never used.

To-day we received the news of the unhappy catastrophe at Laon ; you will have read of it in the papers before you receive these lines. The number of victims which this war demands is dreadful, and, in spite of this, the English would have us contented with money ! With God's help we shall be able, in a fortnight, to meet every un-called-for mediator with 200,000 men, and yet, with the remainder, be able to finish our war with France. People have not yet learned the meaning of the word " Deutschland," but what is of far greater importance, Germany herself has learnt it now. Best love.

HELMUTH.

Versailles, December 12th, 1870.

Dear Fritz,

We have had as much as ten degrees R. of cold; to-day it began suddenly to thaw. Such an early winter is very unusual here, and people say that it is a new "Chicane de Monsieur Bismarck."

We hear more of Paris from English and Belgian papers by Berlin than here close before the town, where only the Valérien (Ballerien as our people call it) speaks to us. The gates of the city are guarded, and even the troops, who camp between the ramparts and the forts, know nothing of what occurs in the city. We expect another desperate sally, but this will probably be the last. The raw French recruits are beaten in the open field one after another, but we cannot be everywhere; little surprises cannot be avoided, but require to be punished with inexorable severity. When a handful of ruffians, armed with guns and flags, throng into the houses, singing the Marseillaise, shoot out of the windows and run away by the back door, the city has to suffer for it. Those towns which have a garrison of the enemy's troops may think themselves happy. Our relations here are well. Henry is well and in good spirits. I suppose Guste was much pleased to hear that he has received the iron cross. To-night he is to sing to the Crown Prince, who likes to hear him. Herr von Keudell will accompany him on the piano.

I had a postcard from William not long ago. He is following up the Army of the Loire at this moment; he is often cold and hungry, but otherwise well. He has a hundred and twenty thalers (£18) allowance to receive from me, but money is of no use where nothing can be had for it. I hope he will soon have a little rest in the beautiful and rich country of Touraine. Unfortunately he had to leave the fine horse which I had given him, ill, at Rambouillet, and when Henry went there to fetch it, it had been killed.

Helmuth had to be outpost again yesterday. The brave boy always does his duty joyfully. Almost every night the forts fire heavy cannon at hap-hazard. Out of a hundred bombs perhaps one will hit by chance. In the daytime the outposts signal when a shot is coming, for the men to have time to lie down on the ground,

where they have not much to fear from the splin-
ters, though it can never be pleasant. It seems
that the French add daily a pound of powder to
each loading; they reach already as far as Versailles.
Nothing is gained by this waste of ammunition,
and the relieving armies they still hope to see,
will never hear them. Henry and I have just been
to take a large tin box with Magdeburg Sauer-
kraut, another tin box with salt meat, a bag of
peas and two bottles of champagne to Helmuth.
The poor boys will have a jolly evening.

The garde-du-corps has not been in any fights
lately. Ludwig is on the Loire. No news of the
prisoner of war, Count Brockdorff, has come, and
it is impossible to liberate him. We have offered,
through the American ambassador in Paris, to
exchange all the prisoners; we have a stock of
them, more than enough, but the French have so
few of ours that they want to keep them for the
sake of being asked for them. So our offer has
remained unanswered. But, with God's help, the
day is not far off when all the prisoners will be
released. The French now have their Government
in three places, in Bordeaux, in Paris, and before

Paris, for Trochu has, so to say, shut himself out from the city.

My compliments to General Hauenfeldt, Scheller and Gliczinski, and all who remember me. It is late; I must conclude. Much love and a joyful Christmas.

HELMUTH.

Versailles, January 1st, 1871.

A happy New Year to you!

May it bring peace, peace to the whole country, and the peace of God which passeth all understanding to every single subject.

(Here follows family news about the relations on the scene of war.)

Berlin, June 13th, 1871.

DEAR FRITZ,

I received your letter from Kreuth yesterday, and am pleased that you like your stay there. I, too, shall have to go to Gastein for a short treatment. I hope to be able to get away during the last ten days of this month, after the winding

up of business and the entrance of the troops into
Berlin, which takes place on Friday, and which
will last five hours.   It is a pity that you are not
here to see it.   It will be most unfortunate if
the weather does not change.   From Lenné Street
to the Brandenburg gate immense stands have been
erected for about a hundred thousand men.   At
the Halle and Potsdam gates stand the equestrian
statues of Germania and Alsacia, which may col-
lapse in the continual rain if one does not put
giant umbrellas into their hands.   The large Belle-
Alliance Square is occupied by two stands, which
reach as high as the second stories of the houses ;
just the same arrangement has been made in the
squares before the Opera, University and Lust-
garten.   Numerous poles ornamented with flags
and streamers are fixed up along the *Via Trium-
phalis* and *Unter den Linden*, cannon and mitrail-
leuses are placed on both sides from the gate to
the palace ; they are closely packed, more than a
thousand pieces, not quite a fourth part of the
number which we have taken from the French.

The house[1] is proceeding but slowly.   The

[1] The new General Staff-building in Berlin.

balcony is finished and the view from it over the
Thiergarten, which is greener than ever, is very
fine.   With best love to Guste,

Your HELMUTH.

St. Petersburg, Dec. 11th, 1871.

DEAR FRITZ,

It is not easy to find a free moment for
letter-writing here.   But to-day I will at least
give you a sign of life, as it is already a week
since we left Berlin.[1]   There is so much to tell,
that I must keep the greater part till we meet.
But I must say this, that in spite of the many
déjeûners, *dîners*, and *soirées*, we are still quite
well and in good spirits, and that we have not
only been received with the greatest attention, but
with real heartiness.   The Emperor himself likes
to distinguish us on every occasion and to give
expression to his good opinion of our Army.   He
has conferred on me his highest decoration, the
order of St. Andrew.   I occupy a whole suite of
rooms in the Winter Palace, a colonel of the

---

[1] Moltke had gone in attendance on Prince Frederick Charles
to the St. George's festival at St. Petersburg.

General Staff is in attendance; there are daily two dinners with champagne, one is called *déjeûner*, the other dinner; in the evening boxes at five theatres are at our disposal; besides that there are *soirées;* and a carriage with a lackey, a coach, and a sledge, are always ready for us. The newspapers will probably tell you all about the great St. George's festival. There were more than a thousand people and more than a hundred flags in the immense rooms of this palace. We must have walked several " versts " by the time we had followed the Czar through every hall. After the reception, Mass was celebrated; then there was a dinner downstairs for 700 soldiers of St. George's Cross, and a banquet of 500 covers for the Court in a large hall. Yesterday's parade went off well. There were forty battalions, thirty-four squadrons and artillery in the square before the castle, along the Admiralty building, and St. Isaac's Church as far as the statue of Peter the Great. It was not very cold, at the most 6° R., and the sun came out, which is very rarely the case at this season. I had an excellent horse, and everything went off as well as possible.

But there is so much to be seen here, that all my free time, after visits paid and parades attended, is filled up. It is very convenient that the palace of the Empress Catherine, the Erémitage, is connected with the Winter Palace. The greatest art treasures are heaped up there. Then it is a great pleasure to drive in a sledge through the lively streets, the prospect and the Morskaja, etc. There are 60,000 sledges in St. Petersburg. You can imagine the crowd. Everybody drives at a sharp trot, passing each other closely without ever touching. Probably we shall go on to Moscow, and I shall not be back before another week. The Grand Duchess Helena is very fond of music. This evening her Imperial Highness has, so she told me, arranged a quartet for me. Before going there, we shall dine with the Czar, who honoured me with a visit to-day. Everything is done to show us respect; our servants, too, are very well looked after. Augustus goes to see the ballet to-night. Yesterday we heard Lucca as Zerline in Don Giovanni. The carriages wait outside the palaces and theatres in spite of the cold, and one can get away at any moment. I profit by it in trying to be in bed before midnight; on the whole, the night is made into day, and as it is dark at three o'clock in the afternoon, the day is very short. With best love,

HELMUTH.

Creisau, June 22nd, 1872.

DEAR FRITZ,

Your last two letters of the 13th and 15th have arrived all right, and we have heard at last from the other travellers. Henry and Käthchen [1] had gone in search of Ludwig, and had learnt "wat bi 'ne Oeverraschung herutkümmt." [2] After a short stay at Venice they went to Lake Garda, embarked for Bellagio and hurried to Ludwig's house—but oh! here they were received with the word of terror, " those you are in search of have departed ;" [3] where? nobody knew. Käthchen broke out into tears, Henry into loud laughter.

[1] Fräulein Katharina von Wimpffen, a cousin of the Field-Marshal.

[2] Title of a book by Reuter, author of well-known tales in the " patois " of Mecklenburg.

[3] Quotation in parody of Schiller's "Gang nach dem Eisenhammer."

They hastened on to Brunneck—no Ludwig there, he had gone on an excursion to Venice and Trent. Käthchen then went to Klagenfurt to her sister; Henry had a delightful journey through Switzerland and the Engadine, and met Ludwig at last at Brunneck. Käthi was expected there; he will accompany her to Munich on the 23rd, then come here by Prague. I expect him about the 25th or 26th instant. Guste comes on the 28th; Ludwig is longing for home. Hanne[1] is to stay three months at Brunneck. They like it very much.

Brunneck is close to Gastein, but the Tauern can hardly be passed except on foot. Ludwig is thinking of going to Gastein.

My programme for the summer is as follows: on September 6th I must be in Berlin, on account of the Emperor of Austria's visit. My journey on General Staff business will be in Alsace, therefore I had to fix the interview at Mülhausen as early as August 15th. If I go to Gastein at all, I shall have to leave this place in the middle of July.

I cannot get rid of my rheumatism here, it has

---

[1] His brother Ludwig's eldest daughter.

moved from the back into the left leg. Gastein would not cure it, but the air there is strengthening and good for the constitution. The rooms here are very cold, and I may make it worse by working out of doors and by getting warm pruning trees, &c.

Auguste Moltke has become wonderfully strong here, she can now walk as far as the Mühlenberg. The four girls are very happy, and enjoy themselves immensely with croquet, ball-playing, and driving.

All of us greet you heartily.

HELMUTH.

Ragatz, June 24th, 1874.

DEAR FRITZ,

On the 21st I went to Freiberg in Saxony, on the 12th to Augsburg, yesterday I arrived here, and to-day I had my first bath. The scenery here is finer than at Gastein and life is pleasanter. The country is beautiful; a very large building has been added to the old hotel where I stayed in 1865 for the last time with Marie. Close by there are most beautiful gardens with rare trees and

vines in bloom, and the air is scented with
mignonette and roses. I had to take rooms at
the top of the house, and have to ascend seventy-
two steps; but the view from my windows is so
charming, that I cannot make up my mind to
change them for other rooms lower down. On
one side the neat little place is enclosed by a
wooded hill, on the other side by the Rhine and
the precipitous, bare Falkniss. There I must not
be seen, or else I might run the risk of being taken
to Vaduz as a prisoner of war. At Nikolsberg
they have neglected to make peace with Liechten-
stein, so that according to the rights of war, the
Vaduz Army might enter Germany if it liked, and
in my opinion the principality is still in a state
of war with us. In the distance beyond, tower
the heights of the Vorarlberg Alps still covered
with large snow-fields; on this side of the Rhine
which, by-the-bye, is quite ugly here, old ruins
of castles like Friedenstein, Werdenberg, and
Krogems stand out on the wooded hills. Near
the last-named castle, which is still inhabited, a
plain stretches along between the Rhine and
the Wallensee. A ditch, of about ten feet in

depth, or a very high flooding of the big stream, would carry its waters into the lake. But such an arrangement would put an end to the Falls at Schaffhausen, and the consequence would be a dull, dirty stream at Cologne, something like the colour of the Rhine here where it flows out of the slate mountains. It does not become clear till it leaves the Lake of Constance, near the town of that name, like pure green crystal. Fortunately this basin, which is a thousand feet above the level of the sea, is also a thousand feet deep, and is able to receive all the mud and the rolling stones which devastate the upper valley of the stream, and have formed a delta stretching out for miles near the entrance of the river. Its stagnant waters, no doubt, render the air here less healthy than at Gastein. The living is much dearer too than it is there. We are extremely well fed, and can make lovely excursions from here by rail with great comfort.

I must conclude my report for to-day. With much love, dear Fritz,

Your brother,

HELMUTH.

LETTERS TO WILHELM VON MOLTKE.

We begin this part of the collection with a letter from the Field-Marshal to his brother Adolf, Wilhelm's father, which requires the following explanations :—Wilhelm von Moltke was a boy at the Gymnasium at Altona, in 1863, who, according to his own statement, had grown beyond his strength ; and after a severe cold he had hemorrhage. His uncle, who was at that time at Frankfort-on-the-Maine, attending a Conference on the Danish question, was informed of this fact by Wilhelm's father. The Field-Marshal replied that he wished Wilhelm to be sent to Wiesbaden, where he would probably grow stronger in the mild climate, and at the same time he could finish his school studies ; he would pay the expenses, and would be glad to relieve his brother. So it was arranged.

Berlin, Dec. 6th, 1863.

Dear Adolf,

. . . Most likely you are anxious to hear details about Wilhelm.[1] Last Wednesday night he

[1] Born September 11th, 1846. Now Lieutenant-Colonel v. Moltke, present owner of the entailed estates of Creisau, and commander of the Leib-Cuirassier-Regiment, Great Elector (Silesian) No. 1.

arrived at Frankfort after a journey of fifteen hours, well and with a good appetite ; there he had a warm room and an excellent bed. As the weather was bad he had not seen much on his journey, but had slept the greater part of the time. I had intended taking him to Wiesbaden, on Thursday, but it rained incessantly, and I wished that he should receive a good impression of his future abode. I therefore kept him at Frankfort, and, as far as the weather permitted, he went about seeing the Cathedral, the Römerberg, the Gutenberg statue, in short the principal sights of the town. In the evening I took him to the theatre, where Marschner's pretty opera " Hans Heyling " was performed. We left at ten o'clock on Friday, the day before yesterday. It was cold, and the first snow lay on the Taurus Mountains. Our first visit at Wiesbaden was to the Headmaster S., but we did not find him at home ; then we went to Comtesse B. She seemed to think that she had been asked to settle definitively about Wilhelm's stay at Wiesbaden. As she cannot go out, she had made some arrangement through her physician with a Professor M. His fees were higher than I had intended to give. I had to give

up a Fräulein F., whom the Headmaster had particularly recommended to me ; but at all events, I
wished to hear first more about Professor M., who
was said to live well, but rather above his means.
I looked at his house from the outside, it stands in
T. street, the warmest part of the town, surrounded
by the hot springs. Through the middle of the
town there is an iron-covered walk which is over-
grown with the vine in summer, so that it is
always a pleasant promenade. From there we
went to the Headmaster, who received Wilhelm
very kindly. He said there was no objection to
Professor M., though he had not mentioned him
at first.

We then went to the Professor, after having
refreshed ourselves by a dinner at the hotel.
Unfortunately we only saw the " Frau Professorin,"
an old lady of few words, and no crinoline, simply
but tidily dressed ; the rooms are small, but everything was in good order. Wilhelm's room is very
small, with one window looking on to the back, but
it is the south side ; view, there is none. She did
not know the terms, and her mathematical husband
was not expected home before 4 o'clock.

We therefore made use of this unexpected leisure, and of some convenient sunny hours to go up to the Greek chapel which lies on a height near the Waldthurm, whence one has a beautiful view over the Rheingau towards the high cupolas of the distant cathedral of Mayence. We visited the mausoleum of the late Grand Duchess there. On our return to the town I showed Wilhelm the gambling tables, which looked quite inviting. Before the Kurhaus, two splendid fountains in large basins were playing, all round it were numerous gas lights. The Grand Ducal band plays every day in the large hall with its marble pillars. Adjoining this hall are the refreshment rooms with magnificent looking-glasses and rich silk hangings, and reading-rooms; also the four large halls with their four green tables closely crowded all round with gamblers and lookers-on. Deep silence reigns there. No sound is heard but the rolling of the ball on the *roulette* table and its falling into the hole, the chinking of the gold and silver coins, most heaps of which are generally pitilessly swept off by the *croupiers*. In other cases the money is carelessly thrown towards the winner. Everybody tries to appear indifferent, but only the bank is so in reality, as it is certain of the gain, with the surplus of which the greater part of this Eden has been created: the park, the playing waters, even streets and railways.

Of course, the pupils of the Gymnasium[1] are not allowed to enter the Kurhaus, but it seemed right to me to satisfy the natural curiosity of a young man in a prudent manner. He has been warned of gambling now.

At last we met the professor in his dressing gown, in a very comfortable study. He said everything would be ready for Wilhelm, whom he would treat like a son. He seems a good-natured old gentleman. There is also a daughter who plays the piano. As they had visitors I did not see her; but judging by the parents I should not think that she would be dangerous.

I have told them that Wilhelm must neither take tea, coffee, nor wine. The Professor proposed weak tea in the evening, which did not seem inviting. He promised that it should be as weak as possible; but I preferred milk in the

---

[1] Boys' schools for the classical side.

morning and in the evening with good wholesome food. This was promised with the remark that the professor himself needed such. Wilhelm has his meals with the family, lives with them, but has his own room, where he can have a fire. The furniture consists of a good bed, a looking-glass, a chest of drawers, a table, a sofa, which has the advantage of being too short to lie on at full length, and some engravings; and a desk on which he can write in an upright position has been ordered.

We must see how Wilhelm will like it. We might still apply to Fräulein F. later on, if there is any sufficient cause for dissatisfaction. Wilhelm has a letter from Sanitätsrath H. to Dr. P., but as he had packed it in his box we could not take it. Wilhelm will go to him, and if necessary ask his advice. We then hastened back to the station for Wilhelm's things, and not till I had seen him comfortably settled in his new home, did I return to Frankfort, where I had still much to do before I was able to return to Berlin yesterday, Saturday. I surprised Marie, who was playing a rubber of whist with General Gliszinski and some ladies.

I suppose Wilhelm will write very soon, and tell

us how he is getting on. He was quite well and in good spirits, as is natural at his age. He looks extremely well; he is not only tall, but quite sturdy. I hope that in a few years he will be, with God's help, a strong, healthy man. He will soon make some friends amongst his two hundred school-fellows. This dull Sunday, while he is still a stranger there and alone, will perhaps be his worst day.

Now farewell, dear Adolf, best love to Auguste. Don't be anxious needlessly. Times are serious enough for real sorrows. Wilhelm has not given me the impression that he need cause any great anxiety. Marie joins me in hearty love.

HELMUTH.

Berlin, Dec. 13th, 1863.

DEAR WILHELM,

I thank you for your letter dated the 11th inst. I am glad that you feel at home in your little room and with people who, though strangers, have received you kindly. It is a pleasant sur-prise that the professor's daughter plays the piano so well, I suppose you will accompany her on the violin. You are sure soon to make friends with your school-fellows, and it is pleasant for you that Colonel Schwarz is so kind to you. Last Sunday week we had a dull day here, the sky was dark, and it rained, and I thought you would have a trying time and would feel very lonely in your little room, a stranger and without friends, but we are glad now to hear that, instead of that, you took a romantic walk in the sunshine to the Burgruine. I hope that the good climate and the beautiful country will prove beneficial to your health, but you must be very careful with yourself. Dr. Pesch says that you must not only take long walks in the open air, but do plenty of gymnastics, calisthenics, exercises, etc., both in and out of doors; but it must not be such violent exertion as would increase the pulsation of the blood, or the palpitations of the heart.

You must avoid running up steep hills or mountains. There are printed instructions about calisthenics to be had, which you might try to procure for yourself. But the exercises are only useful so long as they are done carefully and regularly, for

instance, during dressing.   Only a short time ago
I had occasion to notice what results could be
obtained by out-of-door gymnastics, when the
monthly list of the reserve men of a company of
about forty fusileer guards was sent in to me.
The regimental doctor had measured the men's
chests, and after three months' exercise this was
repeated; it was found that with all these young
men, who are still at a growing age, the thoraxes
had enlarged one, two, three inches, and with many
of them four, five, and even as much as seven.
Of course, you must not neglect your studies
through attention to your body.   I hope that
without too much exertion you will get your
removal to Ober-Prima[1] at Easter.   When you
have passed the " Abiturienten " examination, any
career will be open to you, and your choice must
then depend upon the state of your health.   Remain a good boy, and you will see that your cross
old uncle wishes for your true happiness.

How do you like the food?   Do you sometimes
long for the flesh-pots of Altona?   Tea can be
weakened *ad infinitum*, but as the asymptote, how-

---

[1] Highest form in the Gymnasium.

ever far it is produced, never touches the hyperbola, it would be a harmless, but hardly a tasty beverage. I hope that good milk is to be had at Wiesbaden. It is a pity that the beautiful music in the Kursaal is so close to the gambling-tables.

We had good news from Holstein. Your papa is well, but he has much to suffer from the political difficulties there. Next Sunday the Bundes truppen (troops of the allied powers) will enter the country, and before Christmas a great deal will be decided. Farewell, my old boy. With best love, your uncle,

Helmuth.

Hearty greetings, dear Wilhelm, from your Aunt Marie.

Headquarters at Apenrade,
August 15th, 1864.

My dear Wilhelm,

Thank you for your letter of the 10th inst., and for remembering me. I am very glad indeed that the state of your health is so satisfactory. I hope that, when you have left off growing, you will be a strong and healthy boy. But do not forget that for years to come you will have to be careful, any rashness just in this period of development might do you great and lasting harm. Much exercise will be good for you, but it must not be violent. We envy you your hot sun, from which you suffer at Wiesbaden. Here we are dressed as if it were winter, we never go out without a coat. During the dog-days we had to have fires several times. It is quite natural that you should wish to see your home again, and in the holidays it would not be difficult to manage it. Your Father and Mother and relations will be very pleased, I am sure. I am glad that you manage your allowance so well that you can pay the travelling expenses yourself. As I see that you are careful with money, which is very important for your future welfare, I should like to give you fifty florins for the journey, it will give you more pleasure, and be of greater profit to yourself. You will receive the money when you are at home.

When do the holidays begin? I thought the longest were during the dog-days.

If you have not made this little excursion before, I advise you to go by steamer as far as Cologne.

In this way you would have the advantage of seeing both banks of the Rhine, and with greater leisure, than you could do in the train. The steamer is very cheap now through competition, you can get out at any place you like, and continue your journey with any steamer; you take your ticket to Cologne. At Coblentz (Hotel zum Riesen, where you may remember me to Mutter Schury) you may send to the Governor and ask for a ticket to go up, but slowly, to Ehrenbreitstein. You can also, without special permission, ascend the Asterstein whence you will have a beautiful view. At Cologne (Hotel Prince Charles) there is, of course, the Cathedral; and a little steamer, which leaves the floating bridge (west side) every half hour, takes you to the Zoological Garden with the largest aquarium in the world.

It will be better, perhaps, for you to travel back by Cassel (go up to Wilhelmshöhe with care) and Schön-Marburg.

Your little enclosure reminds me of the day on the Kapellenberg. How I should like you to take me about amongst the beautiful mountains there! But it is very pretty here too, and especially at

M

Apenrade, which is surrounded by hills covered with beautiful beeches, through whose dark green rich meadows and the blue sea are shining in the distance. No wonder it is so green here, as it rains every day, but if the weather is fine, the country looks beautiful.

As you are sure not to be tempted to gamble, you can enjoy the pleasant things at the Kursaal, the beautiful music, the park and the theatre, without hesitation. It is not your fault that the Government of Nassau has not put down the tables in spite of the declared wish of the Confederate States and the many victims.

I have good news from your parents. Your father is well in spite of the bad weather and the political troubles. I hope that matters will soon be settled, and that he will be able to keep the post which has become so dear to him. Uncle Fritz is still in office, but he suffers much under the course which things have taken. . . .

Now farewell, my old boy, be brave, remember me to your Herr Professor, and think lovingly of your Uncle

HELMUTH.

Flensburg, Nov. 1st, 1864.

My dear Wilhelm,

First I have to tell you the sad news of the death of your Aunt Betty. She died after a short illness of three days in the evening of October 27th, quietly and peacefully in the arms of her husband, without struggle. She had not been able to sleep, and her husband held her for a long time for fear of disturbing her, before he perceived that life was extinct.

Many thanks for your good wishes on my birthday. In answer to your question concerning making the Army your profession, I must tell you the following : My physician, Dr. Pesch, who is also an Army doctor, tells me, that, if he were asked, he could not conscientiously give you a health certificate such as is required for the Army. If, while you are at a growing age, you continue still to take care of yourself and diet yourself strictly, you may become a healthy, strong man. But if you should attempt to undergo the exertions which the military service requires, especially the Infantry, it would probably bring very bad consequences. In addition, we have just had a campaign in which

you were not able to take part.   If we continue to
have peace for some time, which seems probable,
you must be prepared to remain a lieutenant for
about twelve or fifteen years.   This is the average
time for this lowest grade, but very often it is
longer.   During the whole of this time, and also
as a second-class captain, you cannot do without a
monthly allowance, which nobody can promise
you for so long a time.   Meanwhile the charm of
a soldier's life will vanish, if you have to exercise
recruits year after year in a little country town.
For those young men who have the capabilities
and the means of studying, and the latter could
be promised you for a reasonable length of time,
other professions offer far better prospects than the
Military, especially in a small country like yours.
If you finish your studies soon, the universal
esteem which your father enjoys and his position
there, will smooth your path.

If you spent the first year of your studies at the
Berlin University, I should probably still be there.
Student life in Berlin is quieter and not so rough
as in many other places, and you can really read
there.   Later you would have to go to the
university of your own country.

After all these considerations I cannot advise you to join the Army.

If, in three years' time, you are physically strong and healthy, and if a war is likely to break out, then we can consider the question again. The time spent on learning will not be lost, and will be repaid by exceptional promotion, only obtainable in our Army by a thorough and general education. Consider this, pursue your studies with diligence, take care of your health, not by coddling yourself, but by an active and careful life, and God will do the rest. This is my advice in this matter.

My kind regards to your Herr Professor. Remember kindly your well-meaning Uncle

Helmuth.

Berlin, Nov. 28th, 1866.

My dear Wilhelm,

I saw you gazetted as an Ensign in the "Militär Wochenblatt." It is important that you should be made an officer as soon as possible now.

A series of short special courses of instruction will be held for all Ensigns, who have joined the Army since the month of May, this year. They were intended to be commenced on April 1st, 1867, but now it has been settled that they will begin on January 1st.

As you have studied a year at a Prussian University, it will not be necessary for you to join such a course, but you can prepare privately, and by passing the examination for an officer earlier, you will gain time. But you must have the required knowledge and experience in practical service. At all events, even in case you pass the examination, you will have to do more practical service before the regiment can propose your nomination as an officer. It is important that before April or even January you should have a course of cavalry training, to which you must pay the greatest attention. If you think then that you can prepare yourself by private studies for the officers' examination in a shorter time than the length of the courses of instruction, you shall be provided with the necessary means. I enclose the Rules to-day, that you may know what is required.

At all events, it will be a good thing to begin to prepare at once, no matter whether you decide for private study or for the military school. I suppose you will have an hour to spare every day for this preparation. Of course your practical military duty must be considered the principal thing. I shall send you the necessary instruction books and maps, as it is not likely you will be able to procure them at Kreutzburg.

With your general information, I think it will not take you a very long time to acquire the necessary military knowledge. But some private instruction will probably be necessary, and this you will receive best in Berlin. I will therefore ask your Regiments-Commandeur to give you leave to come here when the course of instruction begins at the new Military School. The granting of this leave will depend upon your progress in the practical service. The length of time which you will require for your preparation depends upon the amount of work you can do during the next few months. In every respect it is desirable to shorten the time as much as possible, and it lies with you and is in your own interest to do this.

It was a great pleasure to me to learn that your Captain is satisfied with you in every way, and that only a few difficulties on account of your

great height, have to be overcome. I shall send
you your allowance for the first quarter punctually
on January 1st, but if you are in any difficulties
on account of the unusual expenses of last summer,
you must let me know. . . .

With best love from Marie,

Your Uncle

HELMUTH.

Berlin, December 7th, 1866.

MY DEAR WILHELM,

. . . Believe me that he who does not learn
to do with little when young, will not have enough
with much when old. . . . Only he is rich who
improves his circumstances ; he whose income in-
creases, but whose requirements do so at the same
rate, will be proportionably poor. It is very
important for you to learn to be a good manager,
as you will probably be the chief support of your
brothers and sisters.

It is good for you to be much on duty, and I am
glad that you like it, too. . . .

At your age, and in every other respect, it is

very desirable that you should soon be made an officer.

You will receive the books necessary for your preparation in a few days. See how much you can study without neglecting your duty, but remember the lesson of an old professor, who said, " Only with a pen in hand can one study to advantage."

When you think that you are far enough advanced in your private preparation, you must let me know, so that after a short course at Berlin, you may send in your name for the examination. I am inclined to think that you might try for the examination which takes place on April 1st. Thus you can continue your duty all through January, which is of great importance, especially your riding.

It requires a good deal of practice to learn all that really makes a good rider. One soon gets accustomed to one's own horse ; it is better to try different horses. Your browny has had heavy rations, and if she is not used too much at present, she will soon be round and fat again, and smooth when spring comes, if you spare her a little when

she changes her coat and give her a few linseed
cakes. I did not object to her action, much depends on your seat. It is true that her trot is
rather jolting, but she is easily handled.

As soon as your father can find a substitute, he
will go to Algiers and stay there for five months,
or he may remain the latter part of the time in
Southern Switzerland. Your mother will not be
able to accompany him, as she wishes to remain
with the children, but Uncle Fritz will go instead
of her. He has retired as, no doubt, you already
know, and receives a good pension, and the third
Class of the Kronen Order has been conferred upon
him.

Aunt Marie sends her love. Your Uncle
HELMUTH.

Berlin, Dec. 23rd, 1866.

MY DEAR WILHELM,

If, in future, anybody should offer to pay
your bills—which, however, is not likely to happen
often—I should advise you not to let him wait a
fortnight for an answer. . . . It would be more

polite and also more prudent to accept at once. Though I am not "Tetenreiter" of the second division, I have a good deal of business on hand, and no time left for unnecessary letters, but I can always find a quarter of an hour for a necessary communication.

I see from your letter, dated Friday, 20th (meant to be the 21st), that you have had some extra expenses this year caused by special circumstances. Besides that, you lent money when it was not quite necessary. Polonius warns his son against being a lender, because by lending one often loses a friend. The right thing would have been to have said at once that your circumstances would not allow you to help others with money; only he is allowed to be generous who can be so at his own expense. As young lieutenants are not very much in the habit of paying back money they have borrowed, for the simple reason that they have not got it, both items make the sum you name. . . .

He who spends a shilling more than he possesses is always a poor man, no matter if he has an allowance of 400 or 4000 thalers.

You say nothing in your letter about when you think you will be well enough prepared, after having received the certificate in practical service, to begin your private tuition here in Berlin; and to send in your name for the examination of officers. It will be for you to decide, but it is also to your own interest not to delay the matter, for after the course in the Military School is finished, hundreds of officers will join again, who would be your seniors in the Army. . . .

Marie sends her best love, and wishes you a happy New Year, in which joins, Your Uncle

HELMUTH.

Creisau, June 20th, 1878.

DEAR WILHELM,

It would be a pity if Ella and you could not be here together for some time during the summer. It is lovely now. The two acacias in front of the house are covered with blossom, and the roses too are in full bloom. There are strawberries in abundance, and we have young green peas. The new road where you and I

walked through the thick brushwood in the
"Langer Busch," has been still further improved
during the last fortnight by nine workmen, who
have cut it five feet deeper in some places, and
have filled in the holes with soil ; so that one can
now drive up at a trot. I am thinking of making
a better connection to the upper entrance from
the elm-trees, but in order to do so I shall first
have to buy a piece of land.

I suppose you will be able to obtain a short
leave, as matters are quieting down again in
Berlin. Fritz will, very likely, also spend his
summer holidays here ; and you will both be
welcome. . . .

Under present circumstances, as it is of great
consequence to pass the important laws concerning social democracy and reform of customs
(monopoly of tobacco, etc.), I cannot refuse the
offer, which I have received, to stand for two
particularly troublesome seats, at Heydekrug and
Teltow-Storkow. My only hope is that I may be
defeated in both places. . . .

I wonder if the two Conservative parties, or
rather the slight divisions, will be prudent enough

not to work against each other; if they do so, special committee meetings are of no use.

With hearty love,

Your Uncle

HELMUTH.

Creisau, August 14th, 1878.

DEAR WILHELM,

I have a great wish to read the life of Jesus, by Strauss, but I have also a kind of fear which has detained me from it up to now. I have not much time for reading, except the wretched newspapers. I have all kinds of work to do, and I spend much time out-of-doors. In the country there are always all kinds of occupations, and it is so beautiful here, wherever one turns. The carriage has been ordered. Farewell.

HELMUTH.

Gastein, August 18th, 1882.

DEAR WILHELM,

We must send some news to your hermitage, from the clouds in which we live. When you have a clouded sky in the valley, it is raining up here, or snowing on the summits of the mountains. We have several times been obliged to have a fire in our rooms. To-day, on the birth-day of his Apostolic Majesty, all is wrapt in fog and rain clouds, but we shall soon be consoled by High Mass and the Te Deum at which we have to appear in full uniform. In spite of the bad weather, there has not been a single day without some hours in which we could enjoy this beautiful country. There is one splendid path which leads along the hills up to beautiful water-falls. With my so-called asthma, really heart disease, I have to be satisfied with looking down into the wide valley, while Helmuth climbs up to the tops of the mountains, and the high plains. I intend to leave the day after to-morrow; I shall then have had eighteen baths; I am glad of it, for after all, this place, like most watering-places, is a beautiful, but most tedious prison, to which one has been condemned for three weeks. I shall travel for a week in Switzerland, first to Salzburg, Berchtes-gaden, Königssee, etc.; but it depends upon the weather, for if it continues raining like this, there is no pleasure. If one could only know beforehand! but the weather cannot even be foretold by Klinkerfues' clever arts. . . .

The bell is ringing. Farewell. Your Uncle
HELMUTH.

San Remo, March 28th, 1885.

DEAR WILHELM,

I send you a hearty greeting from this neighbourhood which you know well. Living is not cheap here, but everything is good. Contrary to all expectations, and in spite of the much praised climate, it is very cold here ; out-of-doors and walking it is beautiful and sunny, but in the rooms a temperature of twelve degrees R. is very uncomfortable. We take long walks in the mornings and afternoons. Very cleverly planned highroads wind far up the mountains ; but I have left Helmuth to climb up your Madonna della " Garde du corps," by himself ; I move about more on level ground, between the country-houses and the palaces of hotels, on the *Corso di levante* and *ponente.* Vegetation is still backward ; the pear and cherry-trees are in blossom, but there are not many of them. Roses, which grow here in great numbers, are just ready to burst, and there is a great abundance of mignonette, violets, wall-flower and heliotrope. But the grey tints of the olive and evergreen-oak are not to be compared with the fresh green of a meadow in Germany, or the first foliage of a forest of beeches.

The sea is always beautiful, whether it beats against the *Molo* or splashes quietly on the beautiful *Quai della Imperatrice*. Yesterday we drove to Ospedaletti, near Cape Nero; the big hotel and the palace-like casino, which we saw being built two years ago, are now completed; the latter evidently in the hope of opening gambling tables like those at Monte Carlo. There was nobody to be seen there beside loitering porters and waiters. The whole establishment gives one the impression of a complete swindle and failure. The Italian papers say that I am at Nice, and that the police are looking out for me there. Next week I think of going to Bordighera and to Monaco, by La Turbia. And now, with best love to Ella and the children, your Uncle

HELMUTH.

N

Berlin, March 28th, 1887.

DEAR WILHELM,

The critical month of April has come, without M. Boulanger having begun his march to Berlin; perhaps the weather is too bad, and possibly I may pass another summer at Creisau. . . .

The exertion on his birthday has been too much for the Emperor after all. Ninety-five relations were invited to the family dinner. Neither the Generals nor the Court were received this time for their congratulations, only Bismarck and I were summoned. I received a particularly gracious letter, and the only order that had not already been conferred on me, the Grand Cross of the Hohenzollern set in diamonds. . . .

If peace continues, I hope that we shall meet at Creisau. Your Uncle

HELMUTH.

Berlin, March 26th, 1888.

DEAR WILHELM,

All newspapers have had such detailed reports about the death of the Emperor William, that I have nothing more to add. The new Master of the country does not show any external signs of his severe illness. He has not yet shown himself in public, and as long as we have this disagreeable cold weather, he will not be allowed to leave the warmed rooms. How long will he be able to bear the burden of business that must come on all sides ! . . .

I hope you are all well. Has Muthi been removed, or have his masters called *da capo* at his examination ?

I do not yet know if M. Boulanger will allow me to spend another summer at Creisau. . . .

With best love.   Uncle

HELMUTH.

Berlin, January 4th, 1890.

DEAR WILHELM,

I see, from a kind letter of Ella's, that your family will meet again at Breslau on the 5th inst; but that Muthi will have to return very soon to Rossleben, and Leno to Leipsic. I wrote to her immediately after Christmas, and sent her a parcel to Breslau, with a shawl and a pair of fur gloves. She is my best correspondent, and has sent me a silk handkerchief bought with her small pocket-money; it is the finest I have. Muthi tells me that his report is not as good as he hoped, but I see an improvement in the writing and the style of his epistles. . . .

I thank Jochen and Margarete for their poetical effusions. Jochen Peter, Schwerenöther—und Margrete schreib ich spöter. . . . . .

The Emperor has given me a beautiful golden box for Christmas. Henry has been here; and we had much music. But enough now; best love from all of us.   Your Uncle

HELMUTH.

Berlin, January 11th, 1890.

DEAR WILHELM,

. . . From personal experience I cannot recommend Muthi's remaining longer at a "pension." I, myself, got into a great deal of mischief when I was with my pastors. A boy, brought up in that way, learns many things unnecessary for his scientific education, and other things he is expected to know are neglected. If, later on, he joins a gymnasium,[1] he is often placed two or three forms lower than was expected. But I should think that Muthi has character enough not to be easily tempted to be mischievous, though he would meet with temptations of that kind in every school. Every boy must find the right way for himself, later on in life they will see much more evil. I think it would be much better to keep him at home and to send him to the gymnasium at Breslau, than to leave him with other people. Leno is sure to give you nothing but pleasure. . . .

We have just followed the good old Empress to the grave from the Schlosskapelle to the Friedens-allee; you will see the reports about it in the papers. Our united love to Ella. Your Uncle

HELMUTH.

Berlin, March 7th, 1890.

DEAR WILHELM,

I herewith return the letter of Master Herr Jenrich. It will be a severe but salutary punishment for the naughty boy not to be allowed

---

[1] Boys' schools for the classical side.

to come home for the holidays. I hope the measure will be successful. He is not wanting in capabilities and cleverness, the latter quality he shows especially in his mischief. But he is a good, straightforward boy, and I hope we shall see him again in the summer holidays.

Leno, my diligent correspondent, tells me that Ella will pay her a visit at Leipsic with little Monica; it will comfort her for not being able to go home. It will not be easy to find a horse for Ludwig's weight; you will perhaps have to look for it in the Zoological Gardens. . . .

We are all well here. Yesterday all the children went to the Bellevue garden to look for Easter eggs. The Emperor was very active in hiding a quantity of them in the bushes, and the Empress played at "cat and mouse" with the little party, who partook of chocolate afterwards and came home laden with eggs, sweets and flowers. The family life at Court is charming; may God preserve it so!

The Reichstag will not meet before May. As I am Senior President I have to open it, and I am curious to see what they will say to the new and considerable military demands. Very likely the Conservative party will give up the presidency and leave it to the Centre [1] to settle the Social Democrats, for they introduced them into the House. They will now have to fulfil their promises: Reduction of all high prices, the abolition of all customs, partial disarmament, etc. Their eyes will not be opened till the nation has experienced severe shocks. The preludes have already begun at Köpenick and by the boycotting at Blumberg. It seems incredible that in Berlin, a city of more than a million inhabitants, who have much to lose, only Democrats have been elected, and at Dantzic, Königsberg and Breslau the same thing has occurred!

We all send our love. Your Uncle

HELMUTH.

Berlin, March 26th, 1891.

DEAR WILHELM,

You are right in leaving Muthi at school at Rossleben. Though the course of instruction at the school for cadets permits the entering on any

[1] Roman Catholics.

career, when once the boys are there, they almost all become officers. I believe, however, without wishing it, that Muthi will also leave Rossleben, to enter that career. I should be glad if he took an interest in agriculture. In that case he would have to go through a course in the Agricultural Academy here. We will make up for the clothes he has grown out of, when he comes to Creisau during the summer holidays. When you see him, give him my thanks for his letter from Bankau; I hope, that after he has been moved to "Tercia" as he spells it, he will also get to "Tertia." . . .

You may well ask if spring will ever come this year. We, too, have a continual change of rain, snow, dirt and wind. And I am to go with His Majesty, on April 1st, to join the "Carola" in the neighbourhood of Fakkebjerg (Langeland). Oh, the sea-sickness we must expect after the rich banquet given by the senate of Lubeck!

Farewell; all of us send our love.   Your Uncle
HELMUTH.

Selections from Letters to the Children of his Nephew, Wilhelm von Moltke.

Creisau, Oct. 27th, 1876.

DEAR LENORE,

I have duly received your letter of the 25th inst. Give your papa and mamma my thanks for their kind wishes; I shall tell them in a few days all that your "long" uncles are too lazy to write. Give my love to Joachim, when he arrives at last, after having unfairly missed your birthday as well as mine.[1]

I shall keep your autograph, and hope that it may be shown to you again on *your* seventy-seventh birthday. Your Uncle

HELMUTH.

---

[1] This son was born on Oct. 30th, and was to be called Joachim, according to the Field-Marshal's wish, but after all he was christened Helmuth, after his uncle. A younger brother was afterwards called Joachim.

Written in the year 1883.

My DEAR BOY (Muthi),

You have written me such a beautiful letter that you shall have one too from me.

If you come to Creisau next summer and your old Opapa is still alive, I shall give you another Persian arrow [1] for your bow.

Your parents, sisters, and brothers will soon return now to Charlottenburg, and then it will not be so lonely for you. And in the winter I shall often come to see you again. Christmas will soon be here, and who knows what Father Christmas will bring? Be punctual and diligent at school, and remember your

OPAPA.

Creisau, in the autumn, 1888.

DEAR LENORE,

I thank you for your kind letter. I am glad that your foot is well again. . . . I was quite surprised to see how pretty the country near

---

[1] The first, which the Field-Marshal had brought from his campaign in Asia Minor, had been shot away.

Leipsic is, the Rosenau and from there along the Pleisse is lovely. Are you " Backfische " (bread-and-butter misses) allowed to walk there sometimes ?

I suppose your father is still at the manœuvres and will not see your new home till his return. I hear it is very roomy and pretty, but is situated extremely high.

Uncle Helmuth has gone to Bankau to shoot a stag, if one will be so kind as to show himself.

We have been flooded four times this year; much damage was done in the park, but when you come again, everything shall be in order.

Farewell, and remember your

OPAPA.

Creisau, October 29th, 1889.

MY DEAR HELMUTH,

I send you five marks, for this time, so that you may have your watch repaired. I suppose there is a watchmaker at Rossleben, if not, take it with you at Christmas to Breslau. But another time you ought to manage your pocket-money better, and if you have no money, you must not spoil your watch by over-winding it.

I thank you for your good wishes for my birth-day. Your papa has just left here. All your uncles were here for the great shooting party, when we killed 175 hares, 20 pheasants, 5 roe-deer and 1 owl.

Adieu ; your Uncle

HELMUTH.

Berlin, December 24th, 1889.

DEAR LENO,

Many thanks for your nice letter and the beautiful handkerchief.

Herewith I send you something to keep you warm when skating.   I promise you ice and snow in abundance.

Shall you have to return to Leipzic ?   I thought the boarding school had finished you.

Much love from all of us ; especially from your old Uncle

HELMUTH.

Creisau, October 22nd, 1890.

My dear Helmuth,

I have sent you the twenty marks that you may learn in time how to manage money.[1] If you invested the whole amount in the savings bank, you would be a miser; if you spent it in a short time, you would be a spendthrift; it is best to choose a golden medium.

If money is given to you as a present—later on you will have to gain it yourself—you are justified in allowing yourself some pleasures, but it is also prudent to save for the future.

As you manage these twenty marks, you will have to manage larger sums later on. He who spends all he has, will never get on, he who spends more, will become a beggar or a swindler.

I am afraid you will not be able to come to Berlin as you would have to miss your lessons, or you would be very welcome. The more diligently you learn, the sooner you will have done with the constraint of school life.

With hearty love from us all, your Opapa,

COUNT MOLTKE.

[1] The great-nephew had asked his advice as to the best way of spending the twenty marks.

Berlin, December 26th, 1890.

DEAR LENO,

I thank you for your nice letter, and wish you a happy New Year too.

I should much like to come to your confirmation, but at my age one cannot make plans a long time in advance. I suppose as " Queen in the sleeping beauty," you will be a head taller than all your subjects, like King Saul who was a head taller than any of the nation.

I hope the " Yule-clapp " brought you something pretty the day before yesterday.

As your grandparents are going to spend the summer at Dresden, it will be easy for you to see them ; but in the summer you must come to Creisau to your Opapa,

COUNT MOLTKE.

In Lenore's album, first page :

May all the pages in this book be filled with pleasant remembrances.

Berlin, January 7th, 1891.

COUNT MOLTKE.

Opapa.

Selections from Letters to Frau Marie von Kulmiz *née* Von Moltke, Sister of Wilhelm von Moltke.

DEAR MARIE,

What clever animals foxes are! They always look for the place where I stand when they are hunted, because they know that this is the easiest way of escape ; only the one which is lying at my feet has been specially unlucky. A bad shot is all the more pleased if he succeeds for once, and therefore I look with just pride upon your pretty and thoughtful present,[1] and thank you very much, that you have so kindly thought of me. . . .

With best wishes and much love to all your people, your Uncle

HELMUTH.

[1] The stuffed fox.

Berlin, December 26th, 1884.

Many thanks, dear Marie, for having thought of all of us so kindly at Christmas. Your gifts were adorning everybody's table. I will leave it to Eliza to give you details of all presents. I am very much pleased with the charming and very successful photograph of the three little " Druvä-pfel." [1] The baby looks greatly excited at what is going to take place, Anne Marie's expression is that of careful observation, but Margarethe looks above their heads quite full of understanding. The clever weapon against the flies answers a great need, but it will have to be used carefully, or every fly might cost a window-pane. But it is excellent for clapping on the table. . . .

Muthi admired his bicycle so much, that he forgot all his other gifts. After having tumbled off several times, he succeeded, after a little practice, in riding round the table. The number of presents rather disturbs the enjoyment of the children ; and the quality does not come into consideration. Their special delight amongst the

[1] A kind of little apples, term applied to rosy-cheeked children.

many costly things they had, was a wheelbarrow which had cost sixpence.

I received a fine majolica from the Emperor, with Frederick the Great's portrait by Camphausen; I am sending it to Creisau.

With much love to Kulmiz and best wishes for the coming New Year, your Uncle

HELMUTH.

II.

Letters to his Friends.

To His Royal Highness the Crown Prince Albert of Saxony.

Berlin, May 27th, 1871.

I RECEIVED Your Royal Highness' gracious letter of the 22nd inst., last night, and I have informed His Majesty the Emperor to-day at an audience, of the different points of its contents.

It is His Majesty's intention to invite Your Royal Highness to the festivities connected with the entrance of the troops here, and before June 16th to give orders as to the command of the troops which are to remain in France.

In a few days the Chief Command of the First Army will be dissolved; the first and eighth Army-Corps will be placed under Your Royal Highness' command, to cover the departure of the *Garde du corps* from Paris. The removal of these corps would not mean a concentration, but they would be in *cantonnements* in the direction of the return march.   Rouen and Amiens must, however, remain occupied, till the French Government is able to keep a garrison in these cities.

From yesterday's telegrams Your Royal Highness will have learnt that at least one of the Royal Saxon divisions will immediately follow the first *échelon* of the returning army.   Likewise the 2nd Royal Bavarian corps by special agreement arranged by the Royal Bavarian Ministry of War.

Some of the contingents, not the Prussian, go home entirely, and the greater portion of the others, while two-thirds of the Prussian corps will remain in France.

Will Your Royal Highness allow me to commend myself to Your gracious benevolence?   With profound respect, I remain,

Your Royal Highness' devoted servant,
COUNT MOLTKE,
General of the Infantry.

Letters exchanged between his Friends and himself while in the East.

THE following letters have been kindly placed at our disposal by the daughter of Major-General Fischer, wife of the Wirkliche Geheime Kriegsrat Köllner. To letters written to Moltke others have been added which were likewise found in the posthumous papers of General Fischer, such as those written by the Freiherr von Vincke to his friend Fischer, referring to Moltke's stay in Turkey, as well as valuable details about this period, so important in the Field-Marshal's life.

The following will serve as further explanation:—Fischer, when seventeen years old, took part in the campaign of 1815 as a volunteer in the rifle corps and afterwards remained in the Army. He was an officer of the Engineers; in 1834 he was appointed to the General Staff as captain, and was in 1837, with Captain Freiherr von Vincke (Olbendorf) of the General Staff, and Captain von Mühlbach of the Engineers, sent to Constantinople for the organization and training of the Turkish Army. They arrived there on October 28th, and joined Moltke, who had been there for more than a year. Freiherr von Vincke, as senior officer, took the principal command, and the four Prussian officers began their arduous task, often hindered in a really incredible manner, through want of judgment, laziness and mistrust, with such zeal and technical knowledge, that their work there is still highly thought of, and gives valuable testimony to the in-

tellectual military education of the Prussian officers of the
General Staff at that time. At first they worked together at
Constantinople. In the beginning of April, 1838, Fischer was
ordered by the Sultan to Asia Minor to Mushir Hadji Ali,
Pasha of Koniah, to lend his help in organizing the troops, and
especially in improving the fortifications of the Taurus passes.
The numerous journeys which he undertook for these purposes
in southern and south-eastern Asia Minor were useful for his
geographical researches and the surveys of these countries.
The map of Asia Minor and Turkish Armenia, published later
by Moltke, Vincke, Kiepert, and himself, shows his knowledge,
and the trouble which he took with this work, of such importance to science. However, Fischer's health soon broke down
in the unfavourable climate, and he was obliged to return to
Constantinople in January, 1839, but getting no better there,
in spite of the greatest care of Frau von Vincke, he returned in
May of the same year to his fatherland. He was appointed
officer of the General Staff, and instructor at the War
School ; and in 1847 he was made Chief of the General Staff
of the VIIth Army Corps; 1848, Director of the General War
Department in the Ministry of War ; and in February, 1849,
he was attached as Military Attendant to Prince Frederick
William, later His Majesty Emperor Frederick. When the
Prince had finished his studies at the University, Fischer was,
in 1852, nominated "Inspecteur of the third Engineer Inspec-
tion" at Coblentz, where he died in 1857.

Some weeks before Fischer's journey from Constantinople to
Koniah, Moltke and Mühlbach had been sent with similar
commissions to Hafiz Pasha, the Commander-in-Chief of the
Turkish Army of the Taurus, whose headquarters were then at
Messre, near Charput in Kurdistan. They took part in all the
movements of this army, as Moltke has described them in his
" Briefe über Zustände und Begebenheiten in der Türkey " up
to the unfortunate battle of Nisib on the 24th of June, 1839,

which was undertaken against Moltke's advice. With them was Captain Laue of the Artillery. He had retired from the Prussian Army to enter the Turkish service independently. After the battle the three friends were involved in the flight of the totally demoralized Turkish Army, but they fortunately met Vincke, on the 4th of July, at Albistan, twenty miles north of Nisib.

Vincke had gone, in December, 1838, by order of the Sultan, to Angora to assist the Mushir Izzet Mehmed Pasha in the organization of an army-corps, which was principally composed of militia (redifs). Contrary to Vincke's advice, Izzet Pasha led his corps to join the army which was beaten at Nisib. During the whole of the march, which was conducted in the most unskilful manner, Vincke tried with all his might to prevent the misfortune which he foresaw, but he was most rudely insulted by the Pasha, and therefore went with Moltke and Mühlbach to Hafiz Pasha, who had retreated as far as Malatia (about twenty German miles east of Albistan) where, unpursued by the Egyptians, he could leisurely reassemble his army, and await reinforcements. But meanwhile the Army Corps of Izzet Pasha, driven to extremities by hunger, want and exertion, were entirely disbanded without having even seen the enemy. The four Prussian officers, who had been politely

---

[1] Laue had been (Premier) Lieutenant in the Horse Artillery ; in 1829 he entered the Turkish Service for the first time, but he returned in 1831, and was attached to the militia. In 1837 he again went to Turkey, and remained there with the army in Asia Minor till 1841, when he returned a second time to his own country, and as Major was attached to the General Staff. Later on he was personal aide-de-camp to the Prince of Prussia (His Majesty Emperor William I.), after that Governor of Saarlouis. He left the army in 1857 as Major-General. In 1858 he was knighted, and died in 1862.

received by Hafiz Pasha, remained some days at Asbusu, near Malatia, when the news of the Sultan Mahmoud's death, and the succession to the throne of Abdul Medshid arrived. The ambassador of the new Sultan brought the officers permission to return to Constantinople. This tiring and exciting journey has been vividly described by Moltke in his letters from Turkey. At Constantinople Moltke, Mühlbach, and Vincke, found orders awaiting them from their King, to return to Prussia, and on September 9th, 1839, they left Constantinople, after having concluded their business there.

Bujukdere, February 28th, 1837.

DEAR FISCHER,[1]

I have just received your kind letter of the 31st ult., and hasten to answer it at once by to-day's post. You are wrong in believing that I am not looking forward to your coming with great joy. I never find it hard to subordinate myself to those I esteem, and it is with great impatience that I await the arrival of two such dear comrades as you and Vincke.

I had heard of your orders and also of Mühlbach's, but not of Vincke's. I willingly give up the Chief Command of our little colony—a new East Prussia—though I have had the un-

---

[1] Major-General Fischer.

disputed enjoyment of it up to the present. There is not much glory to be won here.

It is a satisfaction to me to know that my correspondence with our Chief, perhaps also the communications I made from time to time to Forstner, Monts, Borcke, and Prittwitz, are known to you. It will have prepared you in some measure; you will have learned by it that it is possible to occupy an apparently very important and influential position, and at the same time to be without influence and importance. This feeling of uselessness, in a place where one might be of the greatest use, has also determined me several times to ask for my recall. In other respects the journey is very interesting, and life here is very pleasant. Your presence here will break the monotony, and I hope that we shall all strive unanimously to work for the common good. You will soon see that here one has to press upon people the things that are to their own advantage.

We were daily expecting the Russian steamer; she is still, however, lying frost-bound in the harbour of Odessa; but with this strong south wind must be here in a week. Count Königsmark will embark in her a week after her arrival. There is a fortnight's quarantine, and so Count Königsmark may be expected to arrive at Berlin in the beginning of April. It seems as if they were only awaiting his arrival to arrange your departure. About that time the Danube will be open again, and as the steamers only take ten days from Pressburg here, I hope to welcome you in old Byzantium as early as the beginning of May. I very much wish that Count Königsmark would return here again for the sake of the cause as well as for our own. But it almost seems as if it were intended to appoint another successor; will you, please, let me know what you may hear about it?

Will you remember me to your wife, and tell her, by way of consolation, that the plague, which indeed was very serious here last year, may now be considered extinct? After such a severe outbreak there is generally a few years' cessation.

In regard to your outfit, I advise you to provide yourself with clothes, books, maps, etc., for two years; for everything here is very dear and bad, and sometimes nothing at all is to be had. As you will very likely go by steamer, you would do

well to bring your own saddle and harness. I have
bought one set of harness here for fifty florins, but
it is very second-rate. If you can manage it, it
would be most advantageous to you to start by
one of the first steamers, later on they do not
keep to their time ; and you might run the risk
of being landed for a fortnight in a miserable nest,
as I was. You will be able to procure the time-
table in Berlin, or you might write for it to the
office of the Steam Navigation Company in Vienna.
As the steamers on the Lower Danube only go
fortnightly, you must make out your route accordingly from Pressburg.

By-the-bye ! Will you kindly inquire at Semlin
at the Steamship Company's Office for letters for
you ? there may be commissions which we should
be glad for you to do on your way. I shall be
anxious to hear what you think of Varna. Two
uniforms, even one, would be sufficient. It is one
of the anomalies in our position, that we smoke
the pipe with the *seraskier*, and sit with him on
the sofa, while the Pashas squat on the floor. And
again in the ante-rooms, the pipe replenisher
neither rises from his seat when you pass, nor do

the sentinels present arms to you. We shall probably have to appear in uniform on very few occasions, and then the sentinels will receive special orders beforehand. It would be a great advantage to know Turkish well, but it would hardly be worth while spending much time learning it, and in the end understanding little of it. You know what a drawback it is to speak a language badly. And we are accompanied everywhere by dragomans. You would find it very useful to have your own servant. If you bring your uniform with you, it will also be necessary for me to have mine; and I should be much obliged to you, dear Fischer, if you would allow your servant to take care of it. I will gladly repay you any expenses caused by it, with many thanks. As I feel sure that you will undertake this trouble to oblige me, I shall write to my cousin Ballhorn to send you a new uniform for me.

I am very sorry that Monts and Borcke are disappointed in their expectations. But I hope to make room for at least one of them, for as I shall have been here two years next November my request to be recalled may be granted about that time. Please to remember me to all comrades and friends. I hope you will write often before you leave, and I am anxiously looking forward to further news from you and very impatiently to your arrival here. Au revoir, then !

With sincere esteem and friendship, yours,

Von Moltke.

What does Major Brandt say to this affair? and what do their wives say ?

Count Königsmark is bringing some reports with him, which at the present moment may interest you, for just now everything, even the smallest matter, that refers to this country, must be welcome. Remember me to Vincke when he arrives, also to Forstner; I ask him to comply with any requests my cousin may make.

Vienna, November 14th, 1839.

Dear Fischer,

Your[1] two letters of this month have given me much pleasure, they arrived when I was ill.

---

[1] In this letter the friendly "Du" is used, in the former, the friends used the more formal "Sie."—[Note by translator.]

Vincke will have told you that I am already better, and I am looking forward to seeing you again soon and having a chat with you about our Asiatic expeditions. You are right in calling me an uncertain correspondent, for to you I have really been so ; but journeys, illness, correspondence with Vincke, and who knows what else, prevented me from writing, and even to-day I cannot get on. Therefore we must wait till we meet.

I shall be obliged to you if you will kindly make my compliments to our high Superior, and remember me kindly to all comrades.

The invitations from your wife and yourself are so kind and friendly, that I may easily be tempted to accept them.

If I should be far enough advanced in my re-covery to travel in the beginning of December, I shall feel much inclined to go by Munich, Augsburg, Nuremberg, and Hof, instead of travel-ling through the monotonous plains of Bohemia and Silesia. I do not yet know the former route.

Enough for to-day, dear Fischer ; my best com-pliments to your wife. With sincere friendship, your   VON MOLTKE.

Not dated. (From the year 1841.)

DEAR FISCHER,

In your interesting pamphlet about rail-ways, which I have read through several times and always with increasing interest, and which is, in fact, a small catechism on this subject, you say on page 29 that an engine moving at the rate of

4 miles will draw 800 centners [1]   -
3 „   „   1400   „
2 „   „   2400   „

with the expenditure of the same amount of power.

Where has this statement been taken from? is it founded upon calculations or upon trial? It seems so natural with steamers, as with everything in mechanics, that power should be gained in the same proportion as time is lost. Lindley asserts (and also the people at Hamburg who firmly believe in Lindley), that every engine is con-structed for a certain speed and that it cannot increase its power, even by going slower, because the vapour escapes from the valve. I am sure

---

[1] 1 centner = 100 lbs.

this cannot be quite correct, but the proportion of 800 : 1400 : 2400 for 4 : 3 : 2 has surprised me much. Resting on his assertion, Lindley rejects all rise over 1 : 1000. And as we cannot avoid a gradient of 1 : 300 in some places of our lines without incurring enormous expenses, he asserts, it is little better than a high-road, etc. Half of his line runs along the banks of the Elbe in districts subject to frequent inundations, where favourable ascents are easily obtained; his plans are founded upon general truths, but nobody can overlook that they incur an enormous expense. The people at Hamburg allow that themselves, but they are afraid when they hear of proportions of 1 : 300, which they may suppose to be like the balustrade at the *Stintfang*. You would oblige me very much if you would let me know, as soon as possible, where you have taken your note from, and also what your opinion in the matter is. We are so far advanced with our preliminary work, that we are thinking of laying it before government next winter.

I am glad to tell you that your wife is well; I have seen her and find her looking very well.

The news from Vincke is satisfactory. He was obliged to stay behind at Vienna, as you may have heard, and his wife, who had to go to Silesia, joined him at Vienna. Our friend Laue has been here a fortnight. His affairs are prospering; it seems that Boyen is particularly interested in him, and I think he will receive an appointment as major. He has not received the Nishan, and has sent his decoration as Colonel to the seraskier, asking him for a receipt.

There is no other news. Remember me to Borcke and Minutoli when you see them. Farewell, dear Fischer; please send me a few lines about the subject mentioned in the beginning of this letter. In true friendship, Your,

VON MOLTKE.

Magdeburg, Dec. 12th, 1854.

DEAR FISCHER,

I am glad that you have taken steps to preserve our claims to the geographical knowledge of Asia Minor. All our discoveries have been made use of in all the modern maps without the source ever being mentioned.

To push matters further, I have sent your letter with enclosure of the 9th inst. to Vincke, who gives the laws in Berlin. My time is much engaged just now with the new plan of mobilization, and Vincke is, in Berlin, in the right place, he will not be lacking in real interest in the matter. I do not doubt that all will be managed well.

The Russians thought to astonish all Europe, and they might have been near enough in succeeding, if the Turks had not taken matters into their own hands. And now it stands thus, that it is impossible for Russia to succeed. The most fortunate campaign would cost them 100,000 men and would at least require a year. But with only 40,000 French and English soldiers at Adrianople it will be difficult to gain the real object of the war. I cannot imagine that the Russians will make the attempt without the sovereignty in the Black Sea, but the most pious Emperor has lent a religious appearance to the enterprise, so that one cannot see how he will come out with honour, and for the Emperor Nicolas this is no small consideration. I well believe that they would like to use us for taking the chestnuts out of the fire. Russia is engaged in the Caucasus and on the Danube, and must guard St. Petersburg against an English fleet and keep Poland in check. If we join Russia, we must not count upon a single man from them. Austria has to fight against Sardinia and the revolution in Italy, and also to prevent a revolution in Hungary; we have the revolutions in Baden and Hesse and a French Army in the Rhine province. Perhaps the Russians would then help us next year, and we should have to imitate the "gratitude" of Austria. One thing is certain, that for the present the alliance has been declined, but it is not certain whether the *Kreuz-partei* [1] and family alliances will not find a way of adjusting matters, but in such a case it would be wise to give an order of mobilization as soon as the alliance is concluded.

It is possible that we may be sent again to the East. But I should not like to go to the Russian head-quarters at Bucharest. It would be a wrong position after having held commissions from the Porte, and, as for myself, I wish the honest Mahomedans every success against the Muscovites.

---

[1] Party represented by the *Kreuz-Zeitung*.

How they are fighting! It shows that every nation can be brave if the war is a real necessity.

The fact that the Turks are before Kalafat is of no great importance. They will be forced to retreat as soon as the Russians advance near Turtokoi and Hirsova. But with the eyes of Europe upon him the Emperor will very likely immensely dislike the position of keeping on the offensive in Wallachia. If Gortshakoff should advance here with great forces, we should send Omer at once by the shortest way to Bucharest, and very likely bring about a speedy return. If Omer would only avoid a big *bataille rangée!* Such a one might be dangerous.

I have hardly any of my works about Turkey left. The original surveys I have given to the General Staff, where they have been partly mislaid. I have only one plan of the places along the coast, the Danube fortresses and the Balkan passes in $\frac{1}{50000}$ reduction. But I have nothing about Varna, and I should be very much pleased if you could send me a copy of my map on oil-paper. My original map of Shumla is in possession of the General Staff. I can have the passes over the Balkan copied for you, but only on a small scale.

Good-bye, dear Fischer, it is time to hurry to a conclusion. I shall ask Vincke to write to you about the matter mentioned in the beginning of this letter. My wife's compliments and my own to your family. Please to give my love to my old friend Frobel, with my best congratulations on his engagement.

Your affectionate
Von Moltke.

Magdeburg, May 27th, 1855.

It was a great pleasure to me, dear Fischer, to hear direct from you once again, though after a long time. I sincerely hope that you have done with all illness now, and that you feel quite well and happy at beautiful Coblentz; one might envy you your being there. . . .

It seems doubtful to me, if I shall be included in the promotions this time. I think for a good promotion it is quite necessary to be in the brigade. Unfortunately I have not done any practical service for a long time, and this loss is not easily repaired. It is possible that I may have already attained my limit, and in that case I would retire at once on the smallest hint.

What is to become of the situation at Sebastopol? It will be of no use to begin operations at Kertch, Balaklava, and Eupatoria at the same time. Omer will not sacrifice himself to liberate the Allied Powers. Is it their intention to withdraw the Reserve Forces to Eupatoria and to send part of the besieging Corps there secretly as soon as possible, so that by the help of a rearguard they may retire from the difficulty with a sacrifice of material only? Eupatoria in itself is a basis for advancement and re-embarkment, but this requires a coast-line several miles long, from which the naval artillery could be effectually worked.

The possibility of success in this expedition lay in the use that was made of the victory on the Alma, and as it was almost entirely neglected, operations will have to be begun again from Eupatoria, which is much more difficult now that cavalry is scarce. A better plan would be to carry on operations from the lower Danube through the very fertile districts towards Kiev. That would make room in the Crimea, but to carry out this plan the Austrians would be wanted. If they are not inclined to move, I think there will be nothing left to the Allies but to make peace. As long as the French are besieging Sebastopol with more than 100,000 men, it will not be easy for them to turn their wrath against Germany or Italy. The time for operations is come, and something must soon be done.

My wife sends her best love.

With true friendship and devotion, Your

VON MOLTKE.

Berlin, Nov. 4th, 1855.

DEAR FISCHER,

. . . The matter about my command is not private and the Prince's Court is well informed about it. The whole affair was arranged officially, without my knowing anything about it, through the Lord High Chamberlain and the Military Cabinet, which had found me suitable. I have

reason to believe that the Prince and Princess
of Prussia have no objection to my appointment.
But what position I shall be able to take
with the young Prince I am not yet able to
judge, in spite of his great courteousness to me.
All his sympathies are with his old play-fellows and
Dutzbrüder[1] at Potsdam and, perhaps also with
his last tried aide-de-camp. At present he is with
a battalion at Potsdam. I only see him at the
hunt, or when he makes a special arrangement for
me to go there. His definite move to Berlin is
being put off as long as possible. But steps have
been taken for the Prince to attend sittings in
the different Cabinets. In my opinion he will
only learn special cases in that way, but it may
be arranged for suitable members of these bodies
to lecture before him on proceedings of the
Administration in general. I have asked permission to attend these sittings myself, that I may
learn what is to be learnt from them.

Besides this, the Prince has asked me to give
him lectures on a campaign. But I have told him
that I would rather instruct him on important

[1] Friends that one addresses with " Du."

military questions of the day, ·very interesting
material for which is afforded by the Great General
Staff. I am now engaged 'in working out the
campaign in the Crimea, and the present state of
this question, in which I am much assisted by
Rüstow's very able book and the collected notes
of the General Staff. It is important not to weary
the young gentleman, but to try to interest him
in the subject.

Vincke has been to see us. It is a good thing
he stays away from Parliament. I think he is running in the wrong direction with his opposing
views; otherwise he is the same old honest true-
hearted soul.

What do you say to Sebastopol? An army
known to fight like the Russian, cannot have good
leaders, and be beaten in two parts of the world.
Since the dwarf of Eupatoria has grown into a
giant, and Kinburn has been lost, I do not doubt
that the Crimea will be evacuated before the beginning of winter even without another battle.
The Crimea is not a place that can be kept uncon-
ditionally like Gibraltar or Malta. The Turks are
too weak for such a present, as Sweden is for Fin-

land. If the Allies were to hold the Crimea, they would have to keep an army there on a perpetual war-footing. I therefore look upon the peninsula as a forfeit which Russia will have to redeem when peace is made. And to that Russia will soon be brought, even without an invasion, by the allied army on the south frontier, and by the blockade of the two seas, against which she has no defence.

But I must conclude my already too lengthy letter.

In old friendship, Yours,

VON MOLTKE.

Marash, June 26th, 1839.

DEAR VINCKE,[1]

On the 24th of this month we threw away Syria. There was no special surprise, no surrounding of the wing, nothing of that kind, but a lively cannonade. The troops were so terrified, that first the brigade of Heyder Pasha, then the cavalry, and at last everybody took to flight.

In the fight we certainly did not lose a thousand

---

[1] Captain Baron von Vincke.

men, but during the retreat or flight we lost at least two-thirds of the corps. The Pasha and part of the Army retreated to Behesne; the bulk of it will probably come to Marash, if the enemy pursues. Hafiz Pasha had absolutely refused to go back to Biradshik, because he said it was *aib* (a shame), when we were suddenly surrounded from the left (strategically) at Nisib. Whereupon I asked for my discharge and for passports to Constantinople, just before the battle began.

Mühlbach, Laue and myself are well and rode here together without delay from the battle-field. We are still without further news. We shall very likely join you. It is now important to raise an army, perhaps near Kaisarich. Adieu. The *tatar* is going away. If they had held out for another half hour, Ibrahim Pasha might have been defeated. He attacked from Biradshik.

MOLTKE.

Letters from Captain Baron von Vincke to Major-General Fischer.

Asbusu, July 17th, 1839. Moltke has behaved on every occasion as " un chevalier sans peur et sans reproche," and as an able, active and discreet officer of the General Staff. Even when he was ill and when he had better have stayed in bed, he was at his post. He always took part in reconnoitring, and as he was bold and plucky, the Turks took him for a kind of Dali.[1] He is highly esteemed by everybody, and the Pasha has always valued his opinion and advice, though on the most important point he did not listen to him. He now sees, only too clearly, how wrong he was not to do so. I have heard this confession both from himself and from other generals. If we had only remained at Biradshik or had returned there![2]

On the 20th, when the news of Ibrahim's approach arrived, Moltke had been lying ill in his tent for six weeks, suffering from dysentery. But on hearing the news, he rose and he has not had any rest since then. I cannot understand how he could undergo such fatigues. Here he has much improved in health through the rest we have had the last fortnight, but he requires care and change of climate for his complete restoration. We are therefore longing for our departure, which depends at present upon Mehemet Ali Bey, the confidant of the Sultan.

---

[1] Dali, a legendary hero.

[2] *Compare* "Briefe über Zustände und Begebenheiten in der Türkei," p. 366 *et seq.*, 5th edition.

Pesth, October 24th, 1839. We (my wife and I) have been detained here since October 8th. Moltke, who has been ailing ever since I met him at Albistan, and who has been weakened still more through mistakes in his diet and colds which he caught on the journey, and the unhealthy quarantine, fell seriously ill in the night of the 6th to the 7th of October, and since then we have been obliged to stay here. Some days ago he was almost well again, except that he was very languid, and I had already engaged places on the steamer which left yesterday, when a fresh relapse compelled us to remain. Though I should have liked to hasten my return to Berlin, I cannot leave him alone so far away from home, and he has no servant with him. . . .

Moltke is suffering from gastric and rheumatic fever, a natural result of repeated colds and irregularities in his diet, which were unavoidable in the life he had to lead. His state is not critical, but it requires great care, and therefore he ought to be looked after, for we know that he is easy-going in regard to himself and his health. But just now he is quite different, and one might call him almost nervous. There is nothing for us but patience, patience! Especially for my poor wife, who seems to be destined to be nurse for the whole Prussian General Staff in the East, and who is very home-sick.

Regelsbrunn,[1] October 30th, 1839. I put off sending you this letter, which I wrote several days ago, because I hoped to be able to tell you of our start, as the varying state of Moltke's health made us hope that we might possibly get off at last. The day before yesterday we really left Pesth by the steamer in the morning, hoping to remain on board as far as Vienna; and though Moltke was very weak—he had been up a few hours for the first time the day before—we hastened to avail ourselves of the very un-

---

[1] On the Danube, half way between Pressburg and Vienna.

certain steamers, for every day it became more difficult to transport our patient to Vienna, as we were afraid the steamers might cease running. We therefore left on Monday, at six o'clock in the morning; it was raining; we arrived in the evening at nine o'clock at Gönyö, where we spent the night. We had taken a private cabin for Moltke, so that he could stay in bed the whole day, and in this way the journey was not tiring for him; he had no trace of fever. Yesterday morning at three o'clock we left again by moonlight; and passed several dangerous places, only to stick fast at Vagha. We were detained from nine o'clock till half past two in the afternoon; once more afloat, we continued our journey for a quarter of an hour to a sand-bank, where we landed to embark on the *Maria Anna*, which was waiting for us on the other side. This transshipping, which we had not foreseen, as we had been told that the *Sophia* would go as far as Vienna, was difficult and dangerous for Moltke; he was seized with shivering fits, followed by feverishness. Towards evening he was better, and had a pretty good night. The seven hours' delay prevented our reaching Pressburg yesterday; we had to lie at anchor another night, and after leaving at four o'clock this morning we landed at Pressburg at eight, where we were much disappointed to hear that the steamer was not going as far as Vienna. We had to make up our minds to hire a covered carriage in which we left Pressburg at noon to-day. But Moltke was so weak, that he could not go any farther, he almost fainted on the way; and my wife and I held him on our knees. May God grant him a quiet night; and may he be strong enough to go on with us to Vienna to-morrow. It is fortunate that we left, for communication by steamer is now being broken off, and in November weather we could not have gone in a Hungarian carriage with a patient like Moltke. What should we have done if we had gone by Italy or Egypt!

Vienna, October 31st, 1839. God be thanked, we have

happily arrived at Vienna. We left Regelsbrunn this morning
at nine o'clock; as far as Fischament—the first station—
Moltke was in a sitting posture, but then he could endure it
no longer; I took an open carriage for my wife and myself
and left the covered carriage to him, arranging it so that
he could lie down. My servant Franz remained with him;
they followed slowly, while we went on in advance to look for
rooms and to make necessary preparations. So we are established in the "Schwan" in the Kärthner Strasse. Though
Moltke has been very weak, he does not seem worse to-night,
in fact, rather better than he was when we packed him off at
Pesth, and I hope that he will gradually recover if he will only
take care. But he is a patient who wants careful watching,
from carelessness about his diet. I hope the supper which he
took to-day with a hearty appetite will not do him harm.

I am thinking of remaining here a fortnight. If Moltke
should be quite strong by then, we shall, perhaps, travel together; but if this is not the case, I shall advise him on no
account to leave before he is quite well and sure of being able
to bear the fatigues of a journey.

Vienna, November 6th, 1839. Our friend Moltke is not
getting on well, I am sorry to say. He has been in bed ever
since he came here a week to-morrow; he has an intermittent
bilious fever, which is decreasing, but which has made him very
weak. I think he must stay here for some time, that he may
be quite strong before venturing on his return journey at this
season. I do not much like leaving him here alone, before he
is far enough advanced to be up the greater part of the day,
and to be able to while away his time; on the other hand, I
know well that my presence is needed in Berlin.

Vienna, November 7th, 1839. I have just had an interview
with the doctor, about Moltke. He has an intermittent fever,
and his stomach, bowels and bile are completely out of order.
The doctor will give him quinine to-day, and in a few days he

Q

will see if his recovery is likely to be quick or slow. In the former case, which may God grant, I mean to leave as soon as the patient is well enough to be out of bed during the day ; I hope this will be some time next week. But if he does not improve, I really do not know what to do. At all events I shall wait and see for a few days. I am longing to get home, but it is against my conscience to leave Moltke alone in his present condition, unless I receive orders.

Breslau, November 19th, 1839. As Moltke was out of bed, and his recovery, as I confidently hope, is thorough, we left Vienna on the 14th inst.

LETTERS TO COUNT EDUARD VON BETHUSY-HUC.

COUNT EDUARD VON BETHUSY-HUC, born in 1800, was first an officer in the Engineers, then Aide-de-camp to Prince Charles, and from 1835 to 1847 tutor to Prince Frederick Charles. From this time dates his acquaintance with the Field-Marshal, whose wife was an intimate friend of the Countess Bethusy, née von Kircheisen. In 1847 Count Bethusy retired from the Army with the rank of Major, and was then for a time director of the Ritter Academy at Liegnitz, and retired in 1851 to his estates in Silesia. After he had sold them, he lived with his son Dodo on his estate Langenhof, which became his after his son had died the death of a hero at Königgrätz. He died in 1871 at Breslau.

Besides distinguishing himself in his profession, Count Bethusy had intellectual gifts of a high order. As a young lieutenant, he had taken part in the Russian campaign against Turkey in 1829 under General Diebitsch.

As an explanation of the following letters, we may say that the first is the Field-Marshal's answer to the Count, who had expressed his doubts as to the drawing-up of the Prussian Army (May 1st, 1866), against Austria, and principally as to the withdrawal of troops from the southern parts of Silesia.

Berlin, May 29th, 1866.

MUCH HONOURED HERR GRAF,

I have received your kind letter, dated the

q 2

23rd of May, through your son. His re-appointment is sure to take place, for officers are much wanted, and all who apply now must be welcome.

You are right in saying that a strong initiative would be the best. The Austrians are six weeks in advance of us with their armament. However, in spite of it we shall have caught them up by the beginning of next week. Waiting will increase their strength, and during that time the hostility of South Germany will also increase ; it also exhausts our financial means, and has a depressing moral effect. It is a grave thing for our old King and Master, at seventy years of age, to be expected to take the first step in a European war, of which nobody can see the end.

On the Austrian side the First Army corps is stationed near Prague, the Second round Olmütz, the Fourth still in Galicia and Austrian Silesia, and the Saxon Army is ready near Dresden. The Tenth Army corps, as well as the Sixth and Eighth, are concentrating round Brünn. They have 140,000 men ready, and 100,000 more who could join them.

As to our measures, we have thought it wise to direct all our forces against the enemy, who is already in the field, and at present to ignore those in South Germany who are only beginning to rise. If we succeed in defeating the principal enemy, the others (except Saxony) will hardly stir.

Naturally our first drawing-up would look like a dispersion. We must begin operations where the railway enters the frontier. But as soon as our soldiers have done so, this necessary dispersion will soon be remedied.

Nothing is known as yet about the intentions of the Austrians. An invasion of Silesia might result in an immediate success for them. But this shock would not affect the monarchy at the centre. Only operations against Berlin would be decisive. Incursions like those which you describe, cannot be avoided, but everything possible shall be done in this direction.

Let us hope for the old luck of Prussia and the ability of her Army; and that it may be God's will that Prussia should now fulfil the mission which is incumbent upon her in Germany. It will be a serious fight, but it will have to be fought once, and on the whole, circumstances are not unfavourable just now.

My wife wishes to be kindly remembered to you. With sincere esteem and affection,

Yours,

MOLTKE.

Berlin, August 19th, 1866.

During the quiet time which we are having again, I must not omit, dear Bethusy, to send you my sincere thanks for several letters, which I was unable to answer by return, on account of the pressure of business, but whose good counsels I have not left unnoticed.

We could not defend Silesia in Silesia, but we attacked the Austrians in Bohemia, in such a manner that they had not a man left for the visitation which they had intended to pay you.

The campaign was favoured by fortune in an almost unexampled manner, not a single undertaking failed. Everybody did his duty, and your kind judgment as to my part in it, has given me much pleasure, though I must attribute your opinion to your interest in me.

You can imagine with what satisfaction the King has met his members. The public feeling has much improved ; the demand for indemnities has had a good effect, also the annexation of Hanover, Hesse Cassel and Nassau. It is hard for the sovereigns, but a division of land would have been harder for the populations.

France and Russia appear unconcerned about this enlargement of Prussia, and the great thing for us now is to win the affections of our new subjects by good and just government, and to organize their military affairs. We shall be envied on all sides.

The Emperor Napoleon could not have chosen a worse moment for a war, than a time when we have 640,000 armed men. We should even have had South Germany on our side, and if matters had come to the worst, we might have entered, at the same time, into a contest with Austria and France. Then the result would not only have been a united North Germany, but "an "entire Germany."

It is natural that such great results cannot be obtained without great sacrifices; many families are mourning, like yourself, for the loss of a dear one.

Poor Dodo! I was truly grieved for him. Your second son, as well as my nephew, unfortunately came too late to take part in the grand attack of the regiment. At present they are at Raitz, a railway station, north of Brünn. May God preserve them from the dreadful cholera.

The diplomatists have been treating now for three weeks at Prague, almost as long as the campaign lasted, and have not yet come to a definitive conclusion. I heartily wish that we might recall our troops from the unfortunate country, so heavily visited by war, hunger and pestilence.

My wife, who wishes me to assure you of her greatest sympathy with your grief, desires her kind remembrance, and I ask you to preserve a friendly interest in yours truly devoted,

MOLTKE.

Berlin, January 6th, 1869.

I sincerely thank you, dear Herr Graf, for the sympathizing words which you have sent to me in my loneliness, and for the kind remembrance that you have of my poor wife.

You too, have had to bear the loss of a beautiful young wife, taken away in her prime, and your lonely path through life has been longer than mine can be ; and what a hard sacrifice you had to make to your country only two years ago.

After such losses the eye looks involuntarily up to heaven and towards a reunion, for which we may hope.

I remember vividly the time when both our young wives had such pleasant intercourse; they mutually attracted each other by their bright and open-hearted characters during the twenty-seven years of my happy married life. How often have I been strengthened and encouraged in grave and momentous times by my wife's firmness and confidence. She was a real patriot, proud of the successes of our Army and of her King, whom she expressly included in her last prayer. Will you allow an old and tried friend to send you the enclosed leaf; and may I ask you to keep the departed and myself in kind remembrance?

With sincere esteem and devotion,

Your obedient,

MOLTKE.

Letters to the General of the Cavalry, Von Tümpling.

General von Tümpling, from 1866 to 1883 Commanding-General of the Sixth Army Corps (died 1884), was from 1842 to 1848 Captain in the General Staff of the 8th Army Corps at Coblentz. When Moltke returned from Rome in 1846, he too was attached to the General Staff of the Eighth Army Corps, and the two years that they spent together at Coblentz strengthened their friendship. His son, Herr Legationrath v. Tümpling, at Thalstein, near Jena, has kindly put these letters at our disposal.

Berlin, January 28th, 1869.

I thank you, dear Tümpling, very sincerely for your sympathy in my trouble. I know that the kind words you sent me, sprang from a truly sympathizing heart. You had known my wife for a long time, you also knew her open, simple character, her cheerfulness and her firm trust in God's providence; all these qualities have been for twenty-seven years the joy and happiness of my life. She was taken from me in the prime of life, and, apparently, of health, proud of her country and her king, and full of sympathy with all mankind. Her life though short was as happy as is possible here on earth, and I would not call her back. I also thank your wife heartily for her sympathy, and ask you to remember your truly devoted,

MOLTKE.

Versailles, Nov. 3rd, 1870.

MUCH HONOURED FRIEND,

I thank your sincerely for your kind wishes,[1] and especially for your kind thought of my poor wife in the midst of the grand successes of our war. If the Lord is going to grant us a speedy and victorious return home, she will not meet me at the station, as she did after the last war, rejoicing proudly in the feats of our Army. I can no longer share the many scarcely deserved rewards which I am receiving with her who was so patriotic and brave, but I thank God that He has allowed

---

[1] For his birthday.

me to live through this great period, and I hope that we shall finish gloriously, what we have begun so successfully.

The present negotiations with M. Thiers cannot lead to any result. These haughty, infatuated Frenchmen must be humiliated much more before they will listen to reason. There are means enough and more than enough since the fall of Metz, but time is needed for them to take effect. But already the Fourth division is forming the reserve, and the Third will follow immediately by rail. Prince Frederick Charles will arrive at Commercy to-day, and also the head of the first Army under Manteuffel has begun to advance.

The news from Paris leaves no doubt that an opposition Government has been set up there by a revolt, and that M. Trochu has been dismissed.

With best love,

MOLTKE.

Selections from Letters to the Oberhofprediger Schaubach at Meiningen.

Court Chaplain Schaubach was from 1854 to 1856 tutor to the eldest sons of the Field-Marshal's younger brother, Adolf von Moltke, Royal Danish Chamberlain and Administrator of the county of Rantzau in Holstein.

He gives the following account of his relations with the Field-Marshal.

Meiningen, June 22, 1891.

My first meeting with the General-Field-Marshal took place at six o'clock in the evening of the 25th of October, 1856, at the station of Elmshorn in Holstein.

The Major-General, then fifty-six years old, came from Flensburg, where he had just paid a visit to his brother, the retired Royal Danish Major Friedrich von Moltke, and had come to spend his birthday at Rantzau with his brother Adolf von Moltke, the excellent Jurist and Administrator of the county of Rantzau.

I was to meet the General, as yet unknown to me, with my pupils, Wilhelm and Helmuth, and we were to take him to Rantzau in the carriage drawn by two fiery white horses. The train arrived; a slim, tall and striking military figure in Prussian uniform quickly left the railway carriage. After the introduction to me and the hearty greetings of his two nephews, no one will be astonished to hear, that I was extremely surprised by this quiet, simple-looking gentleman putting the following question to me, so striking in the mouth of an officer, " Were the horses safe ? " Upon my assuring him that they might be considered quite safe in the hands of the clever coachman, though they were fiery animals, he said to me in a winning amiable way, yet with decision : "In that case, I should like to propose to you that the two boys should drive on to announce my arrival at home, while we walk the four or five miles."

As I could not possibly delude myself into believing that this walk on a dark evening was preferred to a drive "on account of my beautiful eyes," it was natural to think that the General had become tired of driving, and that he therefore preferred walking.

But as soon as the carriage had rolled away, his reasons became evident. With a certain terseness, but very kindly, he began the conversation : "You come from Meiningen ? " "Yes." " Then I suppose you are connected with Adolf Shaubach, who wrote the book about the German Alps ? " " Yes, he was my father's brother."   " Was ? "   " I am sorry to say that he died six years ago."   " It distresses me very much to hear that.   Please tell me all you know of his life ; he must have been an excellent man."   I did so ; and the remarks which the Field-Marshal made in the course of the conversation were a proof of how he had absorbed the book, and how he had thought about it, in a way which put me to shame.

At the conclusion of this conversation the quiet, earnest and conscientious man began to question me about the two boys, my plan of instruction, and my own education with so much tact and yet so thoroughly that I could not rid myself of the impression that the most ideal of school-governors could not more cleverly call forth the innermost feelings of a candidate he has to examine for the office of schoolmaster.   Not a word of praise or of blame passed his lips, yet I soon experienced, and continued to experience to the end of his life with in-delible gratitude, how clearly and charitably the celebrated man judged the thoughts and endeavours of the young tutor of whom he never lost sight again.

Two things that happened on the following day, his birth-day, have specially remained in my memory.

At dinner, to which several other guests were invited in honour of the day, through the remarks of a retired officer, the conversation turned upon the usefulness of the so-called Senner-horses which are bred in the principality of Lippe. The General's first quiet reply was : "I do not know much about the matter," but soon after he said, in answer to the remarks of others, with that obliging manner peculiar to him : "That cannot be quite right ; " and then he gave such a comprehensive and clear opinion about those horses that I involuntarily said to myself after his explanation, though I had no technical know-ledge on the matter : "Any other man who had known so much about the subject would have believed himself particularly fitted by God for this line of life, and breaking through every hindrance would take the lead of the whole horse-breeding of the present time."

Another trait, though seemingly insignificant, shows the General's reverent turn of mind. After dinner, though his time was but short, he drove for several hours over a moor to look up the clergyman at Hohenfelde, who was then ninety years old, and in whose house he had lived some time when a boy. The brothers did not return till night.

On August 22nd, 1868, the Chief of the General Staff of the Army arrived at Meiningen with numerous officers from the campaign on the Maine in 1866. The following morning, the eleventh Sunday after Trinity, he went unnoticed to the Schlosskirche, where I was preaching ; after service he waited for me at the church door to accompany me home, to the great surprise of my congregation. In one of his letters to me, he who searched in his sincere and straightforward manner for the truth of the holiest things spoke about the sermon I had preached that day, and with a quotation from a letter of his, written to me on October 26th, 1880, the Army Chaplain, Provost D. Richter, ended his sermon at the Field-Marshal's funeral. In this letter the richness of a pure and simple Christian heart is revealed in a way, peculiar to him, which touches every heart.

Berlin, Nov. 10th, 1875.

MUCH HONOURED COURT CHAPLAIN,

An influenza cold, which kept me in bed a fortnight, has prevented my answering your kind letter of the 25th of last month sooner. I thank you heartily for your congratulations, and for keeping a true and kind remembrance of me. Your letters are always a great pleasure to me, they allow me a glance into a mind which, in spite of grievous trials, has kept its inward peace, and has found the support of life where alone it can be found. My nephew Wilhelm, your former pupil, has grown into an able, steady man; you will be pleased with him when you meet him again. He is very happy in his married life, and much pleased with a little daughter that has been born to them. I look upon him as the head and supporter of our family when I am gone, which time, according to

R

the course of nature, cannot be very far off.   With
much love, I remain,

Your truly devoted,

COUNT MOLTKE.

Creisau, Oct. 27th, 1876.

MUCH HONOURED SIR,

With all my heart I thank you for having
remembered my birthday again this year.   Will
you now accept my best wishes for your own,
which is only one day before mine ?   I am glad to
hear that in your parochial work you find a recom-
pense for many misfortunes, and that you are rewarded by gaining the affection of those whose
eyes you have opened to real Christian, but large-
minded, views, as I believe you said in a sermon
that I heard you preach at Meiningen, which
went to my heart and touched me much.

. . . My brother Adolf's four giants are all over
six feet high, and have grown into strong and
capable men who do credit to your education.

With best wishes, I remain in sincere esteem,

Yours,   COUNT MOLTKE,

Field-Marshal.

Not dated.

Much honoured Sir,

It is very good of you to remember my birthday so kindly, and I thank you heartily for your good wishes and kind sentiment towards me. It is a particular pleasure for me to hear from you, who have had so many and such early connections with our family. You too, have had much trouble since we met last time at Rantzau, but you have taken it as God's Providence, having received from Him strength to bear it. It must be a great satisfaction to you to know that you have done good even under difficult circumstances, and this feeling must strengthen and support you, even where your good work has not been crowned by public success. If one remembers how little of such success is due to oneself, but that God works through the weak, it must teach one humility. Your former pupils, my brother Adolf's sons, are well. . . . God's blessing evidently rests on the children of such an excellent father. Judging by the one sermon which I heard from you years ago, and which has always remained in my memory, I shall have

R 2

much pleasure in reading the one you promise me.

With esteem, yours sincerely,

COUNT MOLTKE.

The following verses on Moltke's eightieth birthday, were sent him by the Oberhofprediger Schaubach :—

Ob unfer Leben bis zu fiebzig Jahren,
Wenn's hoch kommt, bis zu achtzig steigt;
Und ob es reich an Ehren und Gefahren,
Ob's lautlos, ungekannt zum Grab sich neigt,
Vom köstlich reichsten Leben steht zu lesen,
Daß es voll Müh' und Arbeit ist gewesen.

Und dennoch, dennoch gilt es, ohne Wanken
In mühevoller, streitbewegter Welt,
Getrost und froh aus tiefster Seele danken
Dem, der hinein in Müh' und Arbeit uns gestellt,
Weil, ob durch Glück und Schmerz die Bahn sich wendet,
Das Köstliche in Mühen sich vollendet.

Dich hat Dein ew'ger König reich gesegnet,
Des Geistes Schaffen mit dem Sieg gekrönt;
Du stehst, wie jäher Schmerz Dir auch begegnet,
Im Frieden Gottes da, dem Schmerz versöhnt.
Von Deinem Leben aber wird Dein Volk stets lesen:
„Sieh'! köstlich Müh' und Arbeit ist's gewesen."

Moltke replied as follows :—

Berlin, Oct. 27th, 1880.

MUCH HONOURED HERR HOFPREDIGER,

My best thanks for your beautiful, warm-hearted verses. You are right, full of toil and work my life has been and yours too. I am near the end of my days, and on what a different scale will our earthly work be weighed in the future world! The value of our life on earth will not be judged by the success, but by the purity of our endeavours and our perseverance even where there was no great visible result. What a strange change will then take place at the great review of rich and poor. We ourselves do not even know what we have done in our own strength, how much we owe to others and how much to a higher will. It will be good not to put too much to our own account.

It will interest you to hear, if you have not done so already, that Wilhelm's wife has been confined of another boy, who is called the " Reserve boy." I know that you watch any event in my brother Adolf's life with the old interest. At Helmuth's the same event is expected very soon. Fritz is studying the profession of a Landrath at Stendal; he is an excellent, able man; and Ludwig manages my estate in Silesia; he is very successful, and I am much pleased with him. Marie has been offered the position of Lady-in-waiting to the future Princess Wilhelm of Prussia, and Luise will at present be the only one to remain with her mother in the country.   I am sure you are pleased with the lovely hereditary Princess of Meiningen. Now I must conclude with best wishes, and the request furthermore to keep me in kind remembrance.

With sincere and high esteem,

Your,

Count Moltke.

Selections from Letters to the Private Councillor of Finances, Scheller.

The Field-Marshal's acquaintance with Private Councillor Scheller dates from his life at Magdeburg. Scheller was Stadt-rath there, and lived in the same house with Moltke, who was then Chief of the 4th Army Corps. They had a common interest in the events of the years 1848 and 1849 ; they were drawn into closer relationship which ended in a firm friendship. In 1851 Scheller was moved into the ministry of commerce as " vortragender Rath ; " later on he was engaged as Private Coun-cillor of the Finances in the Marine Department. The intimate intercourse between Moltke and himself continued up to his death in 1883 ; he and also General von Gliszinski used to be regular players at the Field-Marshal's evening whist parties.

The Field-Marshal always felt very thankful to Scheller for the advice and help which the latter gave him as to the in-vestment of the grant made to him by the State.

Ferrières, near Paris,

Sept. 29th, 1870.

Honoured Sir,

I have several times troubled you with requests and commissions, and have not even taken

an opportunity of thanking you for your kind
help. . . .

One half of the French army has been taken
prisoner, the other has been shut up at Metz and
Paris, in the former place for six weeks, here for
one week, and we must now wait to see how long
matters will remain as they are. The condition
of France meanwhile can only become worse, if
the other Powers do not interpose, which they
would scarcely do in favour of the Republic. Peace
is desirable in the interest of everybody; but where
is France? With whom are we to treat? The
elections which were to have taken place on the
2nd of next month have been adjourned. Then
the country would have been properly represented.
The elections would have been made without the
influence of government officials, without the pre-
dominance of the capital, for we should not have
allowed their representatives to leave Paris. The
wealthy classes, the country population, would, for
once, have had a hearing, but that is just what is
not wanted in Paris. We must let the volcano
burn out by itself. Meanwhile we have taken
Toul and Strasburg, and shall now attack Soissons

and Belfort. Our God has been with us and will be with us in future, we hope.

I trust your son has been sent with the reserve troops, and that he will have the opportunity of sharing in the latter part of the campaign.

My three nephews are all well, God be thanked, though the 7th regiment has lost a great many men. Altogether how much mourning there is mixed with the joy of victory!

With kind regards to your wife, and best love to Gliszinski when you see him,

Faithfully your,

Moltke.

Versailles, Oct. 11th, 1870.

Honoured Sir,

I am sincerely grateful to you for your kindness in looking after my money affairs, for which I have no time. . . .

I can well imagine what pleasure the news of our successes, won with God's aid, give you; even when you lived at Magdeburg, when times were bad, you stood firm and faithful on the side of

king and fatherland.   Oh, if my wife could have
lived through these times, how would her patriotic,
brave heart have rejoiced.   She will not meet me at
the station as she did on my return in 1866 ; but
I think the departed are not so far away from this
world that they can no longer feel with us.   Indeed
it is God's judgment that is punishing this haughty
French nation.   They are not humiliated yet,
much remains still for us to do.   In Berlin too,
they will have to be patient.   It takes a long time
to starve out a garrison, as Metz has shown, and it
is not an easy thing to transport about 5000 tons
of siege battery on a newly constructed single line,
on which, at the same time, reinforcements and
victuals have to be conveyed.   Meanwhile we can
keep the impatient provided with news : just now
there is the occupation of Orleans, and let us hope
soon the flight of the government from Tours. . . .
The cavalry has continual little skirmishes with
the " franc voleurs," which, of course, cause constant loss of human lives.   It is a pity that any
more lives should be lost now that the fate of the
war is decided.

Every day sixty to eighty grenades of heavy

calibre are fired from the forts at a distance of 6000 or even 8000 paces, at haphazard, in the direction of our outposts. In this way six to eight men are wounded every day. This cannot affect in the slightest degree the decision of the war, and is extremely expensive.

The whole situation could not be better described than it is in a letter from a very sensible French officer to the *Gaulois*, which you will soon see in one of the numbers of our Berlin papers. . . .

Thanking you again for all your kindness, and with kind remembrances to yourself and your wife and best love to our friend Gliszinski,

I remain faithfully,

Yours,

MOLTKE.

Versailles, Dec. 18th, 1870.

HONOURED SIR,

. . . The twelfth dragoons have had hard work, and as your son has happily escaped, you have reason to be very thankful. Such an experience is not soon forgotten, and must add to a young man's efficiency for the work of his future life. I

have reason to believe that the regiment will have
some rest at Orleans, the troops are much in need
of it after their continued marching and fighting.
General Chanzy is put down for a time, but
Bourbaki may reappear on the right bank of the
Loire. That will, however, take a little time, and
meanwhile rats will become scarcer and scarcer
in Paris.

From the papers and from letters I see that it
is believed at home, that the reason we do not
answer the hostile firing is out of regard for Paris,
or even because of the influence of people of rank.
That is by no means correct; all that is thought
serviceable and possible is done. Surely we do
not want to wait here any longer than is
necessary.

How long this terrible war will continue and
with whom we shall in the end have to treat,
nobody here or at home can tell. A whole
nation under arms is not to be underrated. It is
possible that we may have a million against us
after the New Year; but in the open field we hope
to defeat every hostile army, and in the course of
time even the richest country would succumb

under the burdens imposed by the present reign of terror of the French rulers.

With best thanks for all your trouble, and kindest regards to your wife, Faithfully your,

MOLTKE.

Versailles, February 1st, 1871.

HONOURED SIR,

. . . You will have learnt from the papers that all the Parisian forts are in our hands. To-day I have looked at Paris from Mount Valérien. The city is now nothing more to us than a large prison of a captured Army. It would have been impossible to bring this army to Germany to be fed and housed. So they are shut up in Paris. Faidherbe has been driven to the north, Chanzy to the west, and I hope that to-day or to-morrow the Army of Bourbaki will be repulsed to Swiss territory. Another captured army would be a real calamity for us. In three weeks' time there will be a new Government, which will be recognized by France and with which we shall be able to treat; and as matters stand, one would think that they would be inclined to make peace. But one never knows what the French are going to do, they like nothing better than fine phrases, and a dozen orators move an assembly to take the maddest resolutions. But I am convinced that this campaign will cure Europe for a long time to come of the fancy for republics. The present Republic has lost one-fifth of French territory and a dozen fortresses, has sacrificed 100,000 men, devastated the capital, ruined the finances and, notwithstanding, missed its aim. Trochu also cannot be acquitted from all blame in this disaster, though I esteem him as an able, honest man.

I have no special news about your George, but he, too, will profit by the truce. . . .

With kindest regards to your wife,

Your grateful and devoted,

MOLTKE.

III.

Occasional Correspondence.

ON RELIGIOUS SUBJECTS.

Pastor Baumann, Secretary of the Evangelical Alliance, sent the rules of this society and information about it on May 1st, 1878.

(*Answer.*)

Creisau, May 10th, 1878.

Much honoured Herr Pastor,

I cannot but approve of the endeavours to unite the different parties of the Evangelical Church, but I am afraid that the common ground, so sharply defined by the new tenets of the Evangelical Union, will be too narrow for this purpose.

There are great numbers who honestly seek for truth, but as yet they have not attained that knowledge which, according to your regulations, is the necessary and right way.

The rules, however, very likely express the right point of view for an Evangelical ecclesiastic. But those who cannot honestly assert that these

S

views correspond with their inmost convictions, should not on that account be called infidels or doubters.

I myself belong to this class, and must for these reasons decline to join the Committee of the German branch of the Evangelical Union.

Thanking you sincerely for the confidence you so kindly placed in me, I remain, with special esteem,

Your obedient servant,

COUNT MOLTKE.

EDUCATION.

As eminent man occupying an influential position, had sent a pamphlet of a friend of his, entitled, "Education for the Military Service," by Dr. H. Stürenberg, now Rector of the School of the Holy Cross at Dresden, to the Field-Marshal· In this paper the author, an expert and also an experienced soldier, states his views in an unprejudiced manner about the importance of gymnastics and bodily exercise for education.

(*Answer.*)

Berlin, May 18th, 1878.

DEAR SIR,

I am much obliged to you for your kind letter, dated April 17th, and I also thank you for the copies of the pamphlet entitled, "Education for the Military Service," by Dr. Stürenberg of Leipsic.

I have read the paper with great interest. It is written in a truly patriotic spirit, and shows that the author must be a clever man, experienced in war, who advocates that while the training at school should provide the pupil with knowledge,

s 2

scientific education, and moral principles, the service in the Army should accustom him to discipline, obedience, self-denial, and provide him with the technical knowledge necessary for a soldier. He distinguishes clearly between physical development through gymnastics and other bodily exercises, a necessary preparation for the service in the Army, and the much overrated exercises and games with the gun which, in the popular view, would allow the time of service to be shortened.

In this respect he refutes very strikingly different superficial views on the subject; and he also shows in the comparison of the Spartan and Athenian education, what is the result of an education which subordinates the whole life to the one purpose, the military service of a nation.

I sincerely hope that this paper may find an extensive circle of readers.

With highest esteem,

I am, yours faithfully,

COUNT MOLTKE,

Field-Marshal.

Herr Raydt, master at Ratzeburg, had sent on Oct. 11th, 1890, a paper written by him about the education of the young in Germany.

(*Answer.*)

Creisau, Oct. 13th, 1890.

HONOURED SIR,

You have had the kindness to send me your newest pamphlet, which I have read with the same interest as the former.

Indeed, the principal thing at school is not what the boys learn, but rather how their minds are trained.

I believe that greater attention has been paid to physical training through gymnastics and games, since the publication of the Imperial decree which refers to these subjects. My wish is that by implanting a patriotic mind in the child, every boy should be provided with a kind of safe-conduct for the period between his 16th and his 21st year, from the time when he leaves school to the time of his entrance into the great educational institution, the Army. My wish is that they should be able to see clearly the senselessness and mischievousness of the democratic socialism into which, as experience shows, they are only too easily drawn during this dangerous period of life.

What pleases me especially in the English education is, that, as you say, lying is not only considered wrong, but a dishonour and ungentlemanly.

I thank you very much for your kind information, and at the same time for your good wishes for my birthday, and remain,

Faithfully yours,

COUNT MOLTKE,

Field-Marshal.

Mr. Ernest W. Smith, Editor of the " Revue des Revues," asks, by sending a paper with questions, which authors Moltke preferred most :—

(*Answer.*)

VOS AUTEURS FAVORIS?

Quels livres ont exercé le plus d'influence sur vous ?

La Bible.

Homère, Iliade.

Littrow, Les merveilles du ciel.

Liebig, Lettres sur la Chimie agricole.

Clausewitz, Sur la Guerre.

| Quels livres relisez-vous avec le plus de plaisir ?
Schiller.
Goethe. | Shakespeare.
Walter Scott.
Ranke, Histoire.
Treitschke.
Carlyle. |

Berlin, Nov. 11th, 1890.

HONOURED SIR,

In accordance with your wish, I send herewith a list of those books which I believe have influenced my way of thinking most.

I remark at the same time that I read the " Iliad " when I was a boy of nine years old, so, of course, it was only a translation.

Believe me, sir, your obedient servant,

COUNT MOLTKE,

Field-Marshal.

CHARITY.

Dr. Sillem, of Hamburg, proposes to found homes for the disabled soldiers of the Franco-German war.

(*Answer.*)

Berlin, March 31st, 1871.

In answer to your kind letter, I beg to say that I shall have much pleasure in joining my co-citizens of Hamburg[1] in providing for our disabled soldiers, but I cannot completely agree with the plan proposed by you.

The requests for admission into the Invalids' Homes have been very few since the last wars. Those Invalids who are in any way capable of earning something can make better use of their time, their strength and the pension which they receive, by remaining in their own homes, where they are more comfortable; those who are quite

---

[1] Moltke had been made an honorary citizen of Hamburg on February 9th, 1871.

unable to earn any money usually manage to pay
their families for their keep and their nursing with
their pension. For those few who cannot obtain
the care and attention that they need, and who are
incapable of earning any money, the existing Homes
for Invalids are quite sufficient.

According to universal experience, the best
way of helping invalids, is to provide them with
just sufficient money to keep themselves. The
funds of these Institutions form an addition to
the pensions and allowances of the State, and
are the means by which private and municipal
subscriptions can best be utilized for disabled
soldiers. These institutions can spend their funds
by allowing pensions (Crown Prince Institution
12s. to 15s. per month), or by granting small
capitals for the establishing of a business which
would contribute to the support of a family.

Which of these methods would be preferable
must be decided every time in each individual
case, according to the degree of capability of earning his livelihood, which the candidate shows.

Most of the invalids belong to the rural population. Instead of increasing the population of the

towns by founding establishments for their maintenance, they would be helped best by the purchase of small allotments. This would require considerable means, but the greater part might remain as mortgage on the land bought for this purpose. The obligation of the owner to pay off this debt in small instalments would have a good moral effect.

In the same way those invalid citizens who have carried on a trade might be helped by the outlay of a little capital, which would enable them to recommence their old business.

These proposals would be less attractive than the building of a home for invalids, but they would give back to society working hands instead of idle consumers, and they would further the material well-being and the moral worth of those who are thus supported.

I remain, your obedient,

COUNT MOLTKE.

INTERNATIONAL LAW, POLITICS, WAR.

Herr Alfred von Moltke, German-Consul General in London, asks the Field-Marshal (on May 27th, 1874,) to become one of the patrons of the Universal Alliance, sending him at the same time a pamphlet of this union, in which a diplomatic convention to ameliorate the fate of prisoners of war is proposed.

(*Answer.*)

Creisau, June 2nd, 1874.

Dear Sir,

I have received your letter of the 27th of last month, and beg to ask you to be kind enough to convey my thanks to Baron von Linden and M. Henry Dunant for sending the " projet pouvant servir de base, etc.," which I have read with great interest.

The endeavour to make the prisoners of war more comfortable in their imprisonment (since it must never be made attractive) is very praiseworthy, and is sure to find much sympathy. But what seems doubtful to me is, if the well-meant terms of such an agreement would be kept under the pressure of war. A convention, as proposed, concerning the treatment of the wounded, already existed in

1870, notwithstanding which many of our medical men who stayed behind to tend the wounded French were led off as prisoners.

The "*projet*" says that any officer who breaks his word may be punished with death. Yes, this is all right, if he can be confronted by the man to whom he gave his word of honour. But what if this is not the case, and his own Government makes him a General?

We have treated our prisoners (and they were whole armies) with great humanity, but we should never have agreed to place them under the protection of representatives of neutral powers. I have some scruples about some of the projected propositions, and in my position I am afraid I must decline the honour of being counted one of the patrons of the "Universal Alliance."

I am very pleased that this matter has given me the pleasure of hearing from you, and I hope that your official work gives you satisfaction. Requesting you to remember me to your wife,

I am, yours sincerely,

COUNT MOLTKE,

Field-Marshal.

The General of the Cavalry, von Hartmann, sends a pamphlet to the Field-Marshal (on February 6th, 1878), in which the doctrinal tendency of the modern rights of nations and the claims of military realism are scientifically treated.

(*Answer.*)

Berlin, February 18th, 1878.

I beg to thank Your Excellency sincerely for so kindly sending your newest pamphlet, which I have read with great interest.

Everybody who knows anything about war, will be of your opinion, that it cannot be restricted by narrow fetters. Its terrors can only be lessened by means of strict discipline, the cultivation of universal morality, and the individual humanity resulting from progress made in this direction.

The clever and thorough treatment of the subject will contribute towards refuting the accusations which have been raised against the warfare of 1870-71, though there were no generals who enriched themselves by booty as in former campaigns, nor cruelties such as are reported from the present combat in the East.

I am,

Your Excellency's obedient,

COUNT MOLTKE.

Herr Karl Friedrich August Hauschild, at Herbergen near Liebstadt, in Saxony, relates in a long letter of February 26th, 1879, his views on the blessings that a decrease of the Army in Germany would bring to the country. He requests the Field-Marshal to influence His Majesty, Emperor William, in this respect.

(*Answer.*)

Not dated, Berlin, the beginning
of March, 1879.

HONOURED SIR,

Who would not wish to see the heavy military burdens diminished, which Germany is obliged to bear surrounded as she is by the most powerful neighbours. This state of affairs is not the wish of the Princes and the Governments, but happier circumstances cannot be expected until all nations come to the conviction that every war, even a victorious one, is a national misfortune.

To persuade people to take this view, even the power of our Emperor would not avail; it can only arise from the better religious and moral training of nations, which again must be a fruit of centuries of historical development, which neither of us will live to see.

With friendly greeting,

COUNT MOLTKE.

SUGGESTIONS FOR THE PROMOTION
OF PERMANENT PEACE.

Privy Councillor Professor Dr. Bluntschli writes :—

Heidelberg, November 19th, 1880.

I beg to send Your Excellency herewith some copies of the Manual "Les Lois de la Guerre sur terre," which has been written and published by the Society for the Maintenance of International Rights, in accordance with the Brussels Declaration, and orders recently given in some European States and scientific literature. The endeavour of the Manual has been to bring the exercises and the interests of the Army into harmony with the necessary principles of right and the requirements of the civil world, and to explain martial law in a manner which may be understood by the simple-minded private and the common workman, yet in a correct and comprehensible form.

The undersigned, as also the reporter and the other members of the Society for the Maintenance of International Rights, would be much gratified if the little work, which is intended for practical use, were to meet with Your Excellency's approval.

With most distinguished esteem,

I am, your obedient servant,

PROFESSOR BLUNTSCHLI,
Privy Councillor.

(Answer.)

Berlin, Dec. 11th, 1880.

HONOURED HERR GEHEIMRATH,

You have been kind enough to send me the Manual which the Society for the Maintenance of International Rights has published, and you are anxious to have my approval of it.

I perfectly honour the charitable endeavour to lessen the sufferings which war carries in its train.

Permanent peace is a dream and not even a beautiful one, and war is a law of God's order in the world, by which the noblest virtues of man, courage and self-denial, loyalty and self-sacrifice, even to the point of death, are developed. Without war the world would deteriorate into materialism. I perfectly agree with that sentence of the preface which announces that advancing civilization will also improve warfare, but I go farther in believing that it alone, and not a codified martial law, will be able to attain this goal. Every law necessitates an authority to enforce its execution, and with international agreements there is no such power. What State would take up arms, because one or both of the Powers engaged in war

have violated *Les Lois de la Guerre?* There is no
such judge on earth. Success, in this case, must
be the result of the religious and moral training of
every individual, of the self-respect and sense of
justice of the leaders, who are a law unto themselves,
and act accordingly, as far as the abnormal circumstances of war permit.

And surely nobody will deny that in proportion
to the progress of morality humanity in warfare
has increased.

Only compare the lawlessness of the Thirty Years'
War with the wars of our times.

One important step that has been made during
our life-time towards reaching the desired goal
is the introduction of a universal military service
which has brought the educated classes into the
Army. Of course the rough and violent elements
have also remained in it, but they are no longer the
only ones.

Two other effectual remedies remain in the
hands of Governments, to prevent the worst abuses,
namely, strict discipline, also to be maintained in
times of peace, and the administrative foresight

T

that provides for the victualling of the troops during a campaign.

Without this precaution discipline can only be maintained in a very limited degree. The soldier who endures suffering and want, danger and exertion, cannot be satisfied 'en proportion avec les ressources du pays," he must have everything necessary to his existence. One must not expect impossible things from him.

The greatest kindness in war is a quick termination, and towards this end all means must be employed that are not actually reprehensible. I cannot at all agree with the "Déclaration de St. Pétersbourg" that the "weakening of the hostile fighting power" is the only right proceeding in a war. No; all the resources of the hostile Government must be affected, her finances, railways, victuals, even her prestige.

With such energy, and yet with more moderation than ever before, the last war against France was conducted. In the course of two months the campaign was decided, and only when a revolutionary government continued it for four months to the ruin of her own country, did the fighting adopt an embittered character.

I willingly acknowledge that the Manual states in clear and short sentences, the necessities of war in a higher degree than has ever been the case in former attempts. But even the acknowledgment by Governments of these suggested rules would not insure their execution. It is a universally recognized usage of war not to fire at an officer carrying a flag of truce, and yet it was violated several times during the last campaign.

No paragraph, even if learnt by heart, will persuade a soldier to treat as a regular enemy (§ 2 ad 45) an unorganized population which has spontaneously taken up arms, and from which he is not safe a moment by day or night.

Some demands of the Manual are impossible, for instance, the identifying of the killed after the battle. Other regulations would need grave consideration if the insertions "lorsque les circonstances le permettent, s'il se peut, si possible, s'il y a nécessité, etc.," did not give them an elasticity without which the bitter earnestness of reality would break the chains which they impose.

In time of war, when every circumstance must be looked at separately, I think only those paragraphs will bear effect which refer principally to the leaders. And what is said in the Manual about the wounded, the sick, the medical men and sanitary materials comes under this heading. The universal recognition of these principles, as well as those about the treatment of the prisoners would be a marked progress towards the aim which the Society for the Maintenance of International Rights is striving to attain with such praiseworthy perseverance.

I am, Sir, your obedient,

COUNT MOLTKE.

The discussion is continued in the following letter by M. Goubareff:

Villa Goubareff at Beaulieu, Alpes Maritimes,
France, February 4th, 1881.

HERR GRAF,

I have had the pleasure of reading in a newspaper the letter which you have addressed to Herr Bluntschli, professor of law in Berlin, in reference to the manual of martial law, which was adopted at the last session of the Society for the Maintenance of International Rights at Oxford.

Having a deep respect for your great intellect, I ask you to

allow me, in my capacity as member of the "Société des Amis
de la Paix" and the "Association for the Reform and Codifi-
cation of the Law of Nations," to communicate to you my
personal views upon the war question, upon the advantages of
peace and the means of obtaining it.

Doubtless it is a great comfort to look at the brightest side
of things here on earth, and in all the vicissitudes of life to
believe that good will come out of evil; but this is an illusion
which cannot be of long duration, we shall all be, in the end,
obliged to bow down before that great power, which is called
truth!   However, there are people who assert that war, this
monster, this crime celebrated in song, which is an insult to
our century and to our civilization, this cause of our financial
failures, awakens new life and new bloom in the transactions of
life, and that the loss of millions of men who are torn away from
their fatherlands and their families frees the earth from over-
population, and that the defeated and oppressed nations, though
they lose their freedom and independence, have compensating
advantages.   Even misery, they say, has the advantage of
awakening sympathy.

But what is the difference between such a case and that of a
patient who rejoices in his incapacity of doing anything,
because it gives him, at least, the certainty of never doing
anything that he might be sorry for afterwards ; or of a physician (and unfortunately there are many such) who rejoices in
an epidemic because it provides him with patients ?   Is it right
to rob one's neighbours to find an opportunity of helping
them ?   Or to roll stones before the cart to increase the exertions of the labourer ?   Is it right to ruin some nations so as
to enrich others ? to set the neighbour's house on fire in order to
have the glory of putting the fire out ?   To make a slave of
one's self to procure the enjoyment of being set free ?

What is the result of all these errors which time has changed
into customs ?   It is that personal rather than general welfare

is most considered; and it is forgotten that personal well-being is dependent upon general well-being, that man is exclusively a sociable being, and that the moral power with which he is endowed is a power whose existence is only justified so long as it is reciprocal; that if this power becomes egotistical it divides individuals, families, nations and the whole of humanity into centres which repulse one another, and which can only preserve their existence by fighting. Oh, these wars! They sweep away the healthiest, and prevent the physical and consequently the moral development of the human race, counteracting the intention of nature which sacrifices the weak to the strong; they increase the calamities that already embitter life, and they cause free competition and free trade, those natural promoters of progress and universal welfare, to be supplanted by lawless Utopias which encourage vice and incite each other to wrong.

I beg to send you the memorandum in which I have expressed my ideas about the questions of the day, and my pamphlet "La force morale." I place great reliance on your judgment, and hope that you will do me the honour of sending me a few lines concerning my opinions, if you have confidence in my perfect discretion.

Will you accept the expressions of my highest esteem, with which I remain,

Your obedient,
GOUDAREFF.

(*Answer.*)

Berlin, February 10th, 1881.

HONOURED SIR,

You have had the goodness to send me a memorandum in which you express your opinion

on the serious questions of the present time, and
you have shown me the honour of asking my
views on the subject. I must restrict myself to
discussing your opinions of warfare from my point
of view.

You declare that every war is a crime, even
though it has often been celebrated in verse; I
believe it to be a last but quite justifiable resort
to maintain the existence, independence and
honour of a state.

With the advance of civilization it may be hoped
that the employment of this last resort will become more and more rare; but no state will ever
be able to dispense with it entirely. Is not the
life of man, his whole nature, a battle of that which
is to be with that which is? and so it is in the life
of nations. Who can deny that every war, even
a successful one, is a misfortune for a nation? for
no acquirement of territory, no milliards of money
can make up for the loss of human life or can wipe
away the grief of families.

But who is able to escape misfortune in this
world, or who can even run away from the burdens
of life? Are not both by God's providence condi-

tions of our earthly existence? Our great poet
makes Max, not Wallenstein, say :

[1] „Der Krieg ist schrecklich wie des Himmels Plagen,
    Doch ist er gut, ist ein Geschick wie sie."

And that war has also its good side, that it brings
out virtues which would otherwise lie dormant or
die altogether, who can deny?

Of course it is much easier to praise the happiness of peace, than to determine how it can be
secured.   To balance the interests of nations
which are so often at variance, to settle their
disputes and in this wise to prevent war, you propose to institute in the place of diplomacy a
permanent assembly of members chosen by the
nations.   I have more confidence in the discern-
ment and power of the Governments themselves,
than in such an areopagus. The era of cabinet
wars belongs to the past ; and to-day there is
hardly a ruler who would take upon himself the
great responsibility of drawing the sword without
the utmost need.   If only governments were
strong enough to keep down the passions which
excite nations to wage war ! [2]

[1] Schiller: Wallenstein, Part III., Act II., Scene 2.
    This same thought is expressed by the Field-Marshal in

In your memorandum you lay special stress upon the warlike propensities of the Teutonic race ; I beg you to go through the history of our century, and to judge if the wars have been begun by Germany.

Germany has won her goal—her reunion ; she has not the least occasion to go in search of adventurous martial expeditions, but she may be forced to stand on the defensive, and she must be prepared to do so.   I sincerely wish with you that this necessity may not occur.

As to the conclusion of your esteemed letter, I have no objection at all to its publication with my answer.   I am,

Your obedient servant,

COUNT MOLTKE.

(LETTER FROM PROFESSOR DR. JANSEN.)

Berlin, March, 6th, 1881.
YOUR EXCELLENCY,
Most honoured General Field-Marshal.   Of those who read with interest and admiration your Excellency's views on the discussions on Permanent Peace, or rather on the ideal significance of war, only very few will have the privilege of

---

the introduction to his history of the war of 1870-71.   Compare " The Franco-German War of 1870-71."

communicating their sentiments on this matter to you. I should be the last to usurp this favour. But just as your Excellency's second letter is being published, my thoughts have been directed by my studies to Kant, whose views upon the matter correspond most strikingly with your ideas and sentiments. As I am convinced that they will be of interest to you, I take the liberty of quoting them, and if, which is only too probable, you should already be acquainted with them, I ask you to excuse my zeal, which solely arose from the satisfaction of seeing a general and a philosopher in complete harmony in regard to the most sublime question of political morality.

1790. Kant. Kritik der æsthetischen Urtheilskraft. IV., 120.

What is it which fills even the savage mind with the deepest admiration? A man who neither fears nor is afraid, who therefore does not shrink from danger, but at once with due deliberation goes vigorously to work.

This special reverence for the warrior continues to be found among those of highest civilization, but they require in addition that he should exhibit all the virtues of Peace—gentleness, compassion, and even seemly care of his own person—just because the invincibility of his mind in danger is evinced thereby. And although in comparing the Statesman, and the General, we may differ as to the measure of the esteem which each deserves, yet æsthetic opinion has given sentence in favour of the latter. Even war, when conducted with discipline, and due respect for civil rights, has about it something ennobling, and when so conducted elevates a people in proportion to the peril to which they are exposed, and which they have the courage to sustain. On the other hand a long peace fosters a mere commercial spirit, together with a base egotism, cowardice and effeminacy, and thus has a degrading effect on the mind of a people.

1793. Religion innerhalb der Grenzen der Vernunft, X. 36.

Note. . . . That man can conceive, and aim at something which he values more than life itself—Honour, for the sake of which he renounces Self; this is a proof of some nobility of character.

1795. Of Permanent Peace.

War itself requires no special motive, but seems to be grafted upon human nature, and is even looked upon as something noble, to which man is inspired by mere sense of honour without thought of self; so that the warlike spirit is reckoned of great value, not only, as might be expected, when war is going on, but also as its producing cause; for war is often begun merely to show that there is in itself, a secret worth such as honoured by wise men, as a thing ennobling to humanity.

1786. VII. 380 . . . Only when civilization is complete, and God knows when that may be, can permanent peace be desirable or even possible for us.

1790. IV. 330. In spite of the horrors which it brings upon the human race, and the perhaps even greater burdens which constant preparation for it entails in time of peace, war is yet one incentive the more for developing to its utmost extent every talent which assists the progress of civilization.

The General, who while discharging present duties yet takes thought for the future, has warmer interest and more lively utterance for the idealism which manifests itself in real life, than the philosopher, who rather considers himself a citizen of more perfect times to come. And thus Kant in the passages quoted above, does not quite rise to the eloquence of which he is capable. For contemplating time and space as mere conceptions, he fixes his mind entirely upon ultimate aims, and disregards the centuries which separate us therefrom. Permanent peace is for him in any case an impracticable idea, but yet he believes in a continual approach to it; IX. 204; and he finds the means to that end, in a legitimate state of federation according to the universally concerted right of nations.   VII. 225.

" We see," he himself says, " Philosophy can also have its Millennium."   VII. 330.   Speculation may calmly and confidently follow him into the future.   But the more the possibilities which he places there as realities, are, and can be but subjective views and visions, the more is it allowable, even if in another sense from that in which he used the words, " to conform the critique of pure reason with the critique of practical sense."   He himself must admit that at the stage of civilization which the human race has now attained, war is an indispensable means of advancing it still further.   VII. 380.

Consequently all those sentences in which he praises war as a means of intellectual and moral culture, retain their value for all those to whom a thousand years are not as one day.

I cannot even claim the small merit of having myself collected the quoted passages from Kant's works ; they are to be found in the book by Dr. Conrad Friedrich, Kant and Rousseau, 1878, page 138, etc.   But I read them with a great feeling of gratitude and esteem for Your Excellency, sharing in this respect the views of all subjects of our nation.

I remain, Your Excellency's
always obedient servant,
PROFESSOR DR. JANSEN,
formerly Master at the Royal
War Academy.

(*Answer.*)

Berlin, March 8th, 1881.

MUCH HONOURED HERR PROFESSOR,

In reply to your kind letter of the 6th inst. accept my most sincere thanks for the kind enclosure of some quotations of Kant on the ideal importance of war. As I was not acquainted with them, I was greatly interested in reading them and having my views confirmed in this direction.

With highest esteem,

Your obedient servant,

COUNT MOLTKE,

General Field-Marshal.

The Weaver Master, Ehrenfried Hessel, in a letter dated April 15th, 1881, explains his views on the question of the necessity of war and the possibility of permanent peace, agreeing with the views expressed in the correspondence of the Field-Marshal with Bluntschli, etc., and opposed to the attacks of the Berlin press.

(*Answer.*)

Berlin, April 17th, 1881.

HONOURED SIR,

I beg to thank you for your letter which shows such clear judgment, and is dictated by much common sense.

The attacks from the press make little impression upon me; they are founded upon—perhaps intentional—misrepresentation, as if I wished for war, because I believe it to be an unavoidable evil.

I am,

Your obedient servant,

COUNT MOLTKE.

Dr. Ludwig Hahn sends a copy of his work just published: "The Army and the Fatherland." (Nov. 1883.)

(*Answer.*)

Creisau, Nov. 14th, 1883.

HONOURED HERR GEHEIMRATH,

I sincerely thank you for sending me your interesting and patriotic book. The publication will be of the greatest value in a time when on all sides and even in the Reichstag, attacks are made upon the institutions of our Army, without which a Reichstag would not exist at all.

For how many years people have talked of German Unity in poetry and song, had national meetings and shooting meetings, taken resolutions, which resulted in nothing as long as " logos " was merely translated by " the word." Not until our

Emperor with Roon created the Army, and Bismarck made the "deed" unavoidable, was there power to realize this possibility. But now again only the word is ruling.

The terms in which you speak of me have given me much pleasure, but have also put me to shame ; I know how much I owe to others and to timely circumstances.

Hoping that your health may further enable you to continue your literary work, I remain with high esteem,

Faithfully yours,

COUNT MOLTKE,

Field-Marshal.

Mauritz Mohl[1] sends two pamphlets (Stuttgart, January 14th, 1878) written by himself. One is directed against the attempt to cause a social democratic movement against indirect and all other legitimate taxation, the other recommends the introduction of a tobacco monopoly. The pamphlet ends as follows :

"I am always extremely happy when I may dare to submit any work of mine to your Excellency, because it gives me the opportunity of showing to the greatest man of all times, the liveliest expression of unbounded reverence and esteem."

---

[1] Well-known national economist.

(*Answer.*)

Berlin, January 18th, 1878.

HONOURED SIR,

I have read with the greatest interest your two essays which contain so much thorough knowledge, and which you had the kindness to send me on the 14th inst.

Your refutation of Herr Carl Mayer is very striking. If he makes a point of the voter knowing how much he pays, direct taxation is not wanting in clearness. With the income-tax everybody knows exactly how much he pays, but he also knows how it burdens him. The fact that indirect taxation is hardly noticed at all, is to me its best recommendation; moreover it is voluntary, everybody can avoid it if he likes, as long as it affects the right object.

One of the most serviceable taxes has always appeared to me to be the taxation of petroleum, but it was defeated upon the simple question of "taxation of light." I even confess to be a heretical partisan of the salt duty, though it is quite a necessary of life. It seems right to me that even the poorest man should pay something, however little, to the Government which protects and shelters him. The poor man who buys his salt by ounces just as he wants it, will not receive any advantage if the tax is lessened or abolished altogether. The state would lose a great income from the retailer.

It is indisputable that tobacco is a luxury and, according to your clever exposition, its taxation would be a great source of income if the state monopolized it. It would be no great burden for the wealthy man to pay a little more for his cigars. And how much fictitious value has already attached itself to them, is another consideration. The superfine cigar is often nothing more than a common one with another label. Many people, blindfolded, do not know red wine from white, perhaps under the same circumstances they would not be able to distinguish between a Havanna and a Vierradner.

I hope that the logic of your figures will not fail in its purpose, and ask you to pardon my remarks as those of one who does not pretend to be an authority in the matter which is so ably treated by you.

U

The expression of your great esteem I can only answer with a quotation from Faust:

„Eure Höflichkeit erfreut mich sehr!
Ich bin ein Mann wie andre mehr.“

And with special esteem, I am,

Your obedient servant,

COUNT MOLTKE.

Moritz Mohl sent the Field-Marshal an article which had appeared in a daily paper and which was written by him (Stuttgart, Feb. 10th, 1887), against "the senseless behaviour of the majority of the dissolved Reichstag." He then continues: "The whole of Germany knows that if France wishes to be crushed again, your Honour would lead the German flag to the most brilliant victories."

(*Answer.*)

Berlin, Feb. 11th, 1887.

MUCH HONOURED HERR GEHEIMRATH,

I beg to thank you for so kindly sending your article. If anything can bring good people and bad politicians to reason, it is words such as you have spoken.

Your much overrated but sincere,

COUNT MOLTKE.

Field-Marshal.

Mr. Sidney Whitman sends the Field-Marshal his pamphlet on "Imperial Germany." [1]

(*Answer.*)

Berlin, January 21st, 1889.

HONOURED SIR,

I have read your study on Germany with great interest.

Certainly every State requires a government suited to its individual idiosyncrasies. A constitution like that of England—secure through her isolated position and gradually developed out of the national character, could not possibly be reproduced on the continent.

France, again, has tried—for now about a hundred years—alternately, monarchy in different forms, Empire and Republic, without coming to any definite result.

Only so recently united as an Empire, Germany is an upstart, an intruder into the family of European States. In the midst of mighty neighbours we are convinced of the need of a strong monarchy, and I have been glad to see that you

---

[1] Translated into German by Alexander.   Berlin, 1889.

do full justice to the traditional " paternal Government " of the Hohenzollern.

I am much obliged to you for so kindly sending your clever pamphlet. I am,

Your humble servant,

COUNT MOLTKE,

Field-Marshal.

Dr. D., of London, sent an article on socialism.

(*Answer.*)

Berlin, Dec. 10th, 1890.

DEAR SIR,

I herewith return with many thanks the essay which you kindly sent to me, and about which you wish to hear my opinion.

I quite share your view that real social progress can only be made slowly and by degrees. *Natura non facit saltum*, and civilization just as little. Above all it is necessary to enlighten the lower classes as to their own interests. That must be the work of the School and the Church for the next century. But we are standing, may be, quite close before the eruption of a mighty movement,

and have to prepare already to face the danger.
Your wish is that the social democrats might take
a less revolutionary position towards " the great
number of the educated poor," and that they should
be friendly with them, because then a blessed
change could be effected without the shedding of
blood.

Do you believe it possible that any judicious,
well-meaning and educated man could guide to a
sensible conclusion the movement of the dissatisfied
masses whose purpose is to plunder and to pull
down?   I fear that he would perish as their first
victim.   It is just against the middle class that the
hatred of the mob is directed.   Look back to the
commune of 1870.   It destroyed the monuments of
French glory, it murdered the priests, plundered
the shops, but it left the house of Rothschild
unmolested.

In every revolution those who have tried to be
the leaders, have always been ruined first.   The
moderate parties have always been carried away
by the extreme.   Of all the men who took leading
parts in the French revolution, not one escaped the
guillotine.   And the leaders of the German demo-

crats begin to see already that it is easier to stir up the masses than to guide and restrain them.

I am of opinion that the much-needed social reform can only come from the higher ranks, through a strong kingdom which possesses the necessary will and power, and such a kingdom we have in Germany.

The taxation of the poorer classes has been decreased already, even done away with altogether, and that rightly at the expense of the wealthy classes. Insurance for the sick and also for accidents is doing a great and blessed work. In a few days the law for Invalids and Old Age Pensions will come into power. The further progress of these state provisions can only be hindered, or at least deferred, by the imprudence of those for whom it is intended, and in such a case a display of power is a necessity.

The law against the social democrats was a more humane proceeding; it was a preventive. Should it fail, nothing will be left but severe repression.

It appears to me then, sir, that it would be

better if the educated poor sided with the conservative elements which support Government in its
salutary endeavours, than that they should make
common cause with those who work against it
and at the same time against their own welfare.

I am very sorry to see from the end of your letter
that you are in very needy circumstances. I re-
gret to say I have so many obligations that it will
be impossible for me to render you any lasting and
effective help.

Yours faithfully,

COUNT MOLTKE.

In March, 1891, a well-known French chauvinist wrote to
the Field-Marshal that " he intended to bring about press-
polemics to see if it were possible for France and Germany to
be reconciled and on what conditions. He had therefore
applied to parliamentary authorities (the letter was addressed
to le Comte de Moltke, député du Reichstag) in order to publish their answers in his newspaper, and he promised to publish
them correctly."

The Field-Marshal received this letter in the Herrenhaus
(Upper House) and wrote his answer, as was his habit, at once
on the back of the sheet which contained the order of the day :

I believe a reconciliation between Germany and

France to be possible, because sensible. The condition is a candid recognition of the treaty of Frankfort.

This answer was, however, not posted, as the Field-Marshal was informed by trustworthy people about the inquirer.

LETTERS OF CONGRATULATION,

ACKNOWLEDGMENT, etc.

To Count von Egloffstein at Arklitten in East Prussia.

Berlin, August 25th, 1866.

DEAR SIR,

I thank you sincerely for having so kindly remembered a younger comrade of the General Staff. I have read with great interest your "parting words," and I hope that before your actual departure your heart has been gladdened by the valour of the grandchildren of those heroes who fought by your side during the wars of liberation.

The death of brave Königer, a real Prussian at heart, and whose fate it was to die pierced by Prussian bullets in the fight against Prussia, is a proof of the untenable position of Germany. My

---

[1] Count von Egloffstein's letter, which was the occasion of this letter, is not forthcoming.

attention had been drawn to Königer by his excellent essays. I was in correspondence with him, and hoped to have him for the war-history section of the General Staff as soon as my staff was enlarged.

In reference to your kind mention of my part in the last successful events of the war, I may say that these words have often come into my mind: "The Lord is strong in the weak."

Please to accept the assurance of my most sincere esteem, and believe me to remain,

Yours Faithfully,

MOLTKE,

General and Chief of the

General Staff.

Count Egloffstein writes on January 16th, 1881 :—

It is the heartfelt wish of a veteran of eighty-five to offer to Your Excellency a visible proof of his good wishes and blessings, before he is called away by God Almighty.

I have given to my nephew, who enjoys the honour and happiness of being under Your Excellency's command and leadership, the letter which you once wrote to me after God had done so much through you, and when you gave Him thanks for what He had done. That is the most beautiful leaf in Your Excellency's wreath of laurels.

Will you kindly remember a veteran and tired pilgrim, who is preparing for the grand recall ?

(*Answer.*)

Berlin, January 25th, 1881.

HONOURED HERR GRAF,

Please to accept my heartiest thanks for your kind lines, dated 16th inst., which were delivered to me by your nephew. According to God's gracious providence both of us have reached old age, I being only four years behind you, and must both be prepared to be called away soon ; may God be a gracious judge to us.

With best wishes and true esteem, I remain,

Your obedient servant,

COUNT MOLTKE,

Field-Marshal.

The General of the Cavalry, Baron von Manteuffel, sends his good wishes for the New Year. (Nancy, December 30th, 1871.)

(*Answer.*)

Berlin, January 3rd, 1872.

I sincerely thank your Excellency for the kind lines of the 30th of last month, and beg you to accept my best wishes for the New Year. May it bring more light to the world, and make even enemies and malicious enviers see the great things you have done for King and Fatherland. The unprejudiced and well-informed can appreciate them already, but the blind majority will be more influenced by the relation of them in history than in the press.

May God keep you in good health and in unabated strength in your important place.

With sincere esteem,

Count Moltke.

The North American historian and statesman, George Bancroft, from 1867 to 1874 ambassador in Berlin, wrote on February 18th, 1885 :—

We were born in the same month of the same year. I am twenty-three days older than you. I am in excellent health, and hope to hear the same of you. The remembrance of our friendship during my stay in Berlin is still a joy to me in my old age. I keep my former opinion that the union of Germany is the greatest event of our century. My wife, who, I am glad to say, is in good health, joins me in best wishes.

(*Answer.*)

Berlin, March 3rd, 1885.

I am glad to learn from your Excellency's kind

letter of the 18th of last month, that you still wish me well even on the other side of the ocean.

From time to time I hear news of you from your countrymen, and I hear that your activity enables you to continue the rides, in which I so often had the honour of accompanying you here.

The high significance which you rightfully attach to the union of Germany, whose friend you have always shown yourself, is certainly justified; I think that a powerful and yet peaceable state in the heart of Europe is the greatest security for lasting tranquillity in this part of the world.

May you retain, for many years to come, the twenty-three days by which you are in advance of me,[1] and asking you to give my kindest regards to your wife,

I remain, your most devoted,
COUNT MOLTKE.

As an example of the Field-Marshal's terse eloquence we give here the following toast, which he gave at a farewell dinner

---

[1] Bancroft died on January 17th, 1890, at Washington.

of the officers of the Great General Staff in honour of a departing comrade in the year 1883.

To-day, when our guest is leaving our circle to occupy a high place as Commander in the Army, we remember the many years during which he has belonged to us. Many of you, gentlemen, honour in him a master and leader, all of us a genial superior, and amiable comrade. To me he has been a faithful companion in two campaigns, and a firm support in peace. While uniting our good wishes for his future let us join in a hearty cheer. " Hurrah ! "

VARIOUS PROOFS OF ESTEEM.

THE Directors of the Berlin Anhalter Railway Company asked for permission to give the name of "Moltke" to a new engine.

(*Answer.*)

(Place not named), April 13th, 1872.

I beg to thank the honoured directors for the intended compliment. I hope that the engine which will bear my name may traverse as great distances as I have done during my life with God's gracious help.

COUNT MOLTKE.

Nominated a member of the Imperial Russian Academy of Science at St. Petersburg.

From the President of the Imperial Academy of Science at St. Petersburg.

December 5th (17th), 1871.

To His Excellency Count Helmuth von Moltke, Field-Marshal and Knight of sublime orders.

ILLUSTRIOUS COUNT,

The decisive part which your Excellency has taken in the recent historical events which have insured the triumph of true civilization, has engraved your name for ever in the annals of history. Will your Excellency permit your glorious name to be added to the list in the Imperial Academy of Science, to leave a testimony to coming generations of the admiring recognition of your great deeds? Requesting you to accept the enclosed diploma of an honorary member of the Imperial Academy of Science,

I remain, your Excellency's
Obedient Servant,
COUNT FR. LÜTKE,
President.

(*Acknowledgment.*)

To the President of the Imperial Russian Academy of Science, Knight of the highest orders.

The Admiral Count Lütke, Excellency.

Berlin, December 24th, 1871.

I am sorry not to have found your Excellency at home, when I paid you my farewell visit at St. Petersburg; will you, therefore, allow me now to express my sincere thanks to you for the distinction which has been conferred on me by my admission to the Imperial Academy of Science. I esteem it a special honour to see my name recorded with those whose scientific reputations are known throughout the world. Besides the enormous progress that true humanity has made in the vast realm of Russia during the last decade and a half, these splendid institutions for Science and Art show the attention paid to the highest intellectual development.

I beg to express to your Excellency, as the worthy promoter of progress in this department, the high esteem with which I remain,

Your Excellency's obedient servant,

CeCOUNT MOLTKE,
Field-Marshal.

LITERARY HOMAGE.

HOFFMANN VON FALLERSLEBEN sends the following lines :—

For the 26th of October, 1873.

Wem gilt am heutigen Tage
Des Dankes Sang und Wort?
Ein Held ist heute geboren,
Gott hat ihn auserkoren
Zu Deutschlands Segenshort.

Das bist Du, edler Moltke!
Dank Dir viel tausendmal!
Du kriegserfahrener Denker
Du sicherer Schlachtenlenker,
Du glücklicher General.

Du hast das Volk, das nur dachte,
Zum Thatenvolk gemacht;
Den Sieg stets vorbereitet,
Zu Ruhm und Ehr' uns geleitet
Durch manche glückliche Schlacht.

So sei denn heut' und immer
Herzinnig Deiner gedacht.
Und noch in fernen Tagen
Soll Deutschland singen und sagen
Was Du für uns vollbracht.

Schloß Corvey.   Hoffmann von Fallersleben.

(Acknowledgment.)

Creisau, Oct. 26th, 1873.

My heartiest thanks to the celebrated poet at Schloss Corvey for the verses, which no other but himself could have written.

COUNT MOLTKE.

Professor Dr. Felix Dahn had sent for the Field-Marshal's ninetieth birthday his play "Moltke" (first part: at Walhalla, 1870; second and principal part: in Moltke's camp, 1870; third part: conclusion, 1890), and other poetry of his, dedicated to the Field-Marshal.

To Professor Felix Dahn in Berlin.

Creisau, Oct. 17th, 1890.

MUCH HONOURED HERR PROFESSOR,

It is a great honour for me that my approaching birthday has caused a man of your high literary fame to celebrate my actions in your play and your beautiful verses, though I feel that my merits are far too small to be deserving of it. The good opinion of me which you reveal in these works, is all the more valuable to me as it is that of a writer who has given me many happy hours by his works, especially by the "Kampf um Rom."

Will you accept, dear Sir, my most sincere

thanks for your writings as well as for the amiable expressions which accompanied them?

Your obedient Servant,

COUNT MOLTKE,

Field-Marshal.

A young lady belonging to the Alsacian aristocracy had written a number of poems which celebrated " The Life and Deeds of the Field-Marshal." She made inquiry through a friend, if the Field-Marshal would condescend to see the poems and allow her to dedicate them to him.

(*Answer.*)

Creisau, June 20th, 1877.

I fully appreciate the compliment paid to me by a young lady writing poetry in my honour. But in such a case a special dedication would not be necessary, and I think I would rather decline the offer with thanks.

My life has hardly been poetical enough, and I must confess that I should much prefer all remarks on me to be postponed to a distant future.

COUNT MOLTKE.

A publishing firm, which was preparing a biography of the Field-Marshal, asked for kind information for the use of the author.

(*Answer*.)

Creisau, July, 20th, 1877.

I gratefully recognize the kind intention, but I take the liberty of remarking that biographies of living men can hardly be anything else but so many panegyrics, which everybody puts aside as tedious. An impartial judgment must be left till after the death of the person in question.

Fate willed that I was not to be placed in such circumstances as to excite universal interest till I was advanced in age. Nobody would be interested in my earlier years. All that is at all noteworthy of this period is already known through letters which have been published.

The character of a man is a riddle difficult to solve, even for his relations, how much more so for strangers. Herr[1] . . . would not be able to give a true picture of me, even if he could build on the uncertain foundation of personal acquaintance.

I should like to leave it to posterity to give its opinion about me, and as the work has luckily not been begun yet, I can only sincerely hope the idea will be abandoned.

COUNT MOLTKE.

[1] The author.